NOT FOR THE NIGHT-TIME

NOT FOR THE NIGHT-TIME

THEO GIFT

WILDSIDE PRESS

Published by Wildside Press LLC.
wildsidepress.com | bcmystery.com

CONTENTS.

WHAT WAS HE?

CHAPTER I.

NOT EXPLAINED.

PART I.

'DOG OR DEMON?'

INTRODUCTION

Theo Gift was the pseudonym of Dorothy Havers (1854-1923), a British novelist and short story writer. She is best remembered today for her supernatural fiction and her children's tales, especially those set in the Falkland Islands.

She was born at Thelton Hall, Norfolk, daughter of Thomas Havers and Ellen Ruding. In 1854, she moved with her parents to the Falkland Islands, where her father was manager of the Falkland Islands Company. Her mother died in Stanley, at which point her father married Dorothy's governess.

In 1861, the family moved to Montevideo, where they lived until her father's death 1870, whereupon the surviving family returned to England. There, Dorothy Havers began to write stories for magazines and published her first novel in 1874. Those early novels are contemporary romances, and the influence of her family's Catholicism is more pronounced there than in her later works.

As she wrote under the name of Theo Gift, some reviewers believed she was a man. *Maid Ellice*, which she wrote in 1878, is semi-autobiographical, about an orphaned girl from Montevideo moving to England and the contrast with her upbringing in Uruguay.

In 1879 she married George Simonds Boulger, an eminent botanist. After their marriage, she wrote another autobiographical work, *Lil Lorimer*, and a book for children, *Cape Town Dicky* (illustrated by her sister Alice Havers, who was an accomplished artist).

During the 1890s she wrote two books of fiction for girls set in the Falkland Islands: *The Little Colonists* (1890) and *An Island Princess* (1893). These give a vivid picture of the isolated life of the colonists and include detailed descriptions of islands. She does not evade difficult topics like alcoholism or over-zealous missionaries.

Much of her work—including some of the stories in this collection—show independent minded young women. Clearly she was an early feminist author, and her work needs to be rediscovered and explored in this light.

—Karl Wurf
Rockville, MD
August 15, 2020

WHAT WAS HE?

CHAPTER I.

THE FIRST TIME.

I THINK it was in the second week of August, 1868, that it happened. I may not be quite right about the time of the month or the month itself; but I am almost sure it was in August; and I know it was that summer, the summer of 1868, that I spent in Switzerland. If I make any mistakes, or there are found any discrepancies in this narrative, I hope the critics will excuse them, and not say sharp things about me, as they do of regular story-writers. I say at once, I do not know how to write a story at all, and have never done such a thing before in my life; but those who have heard the account of these three painful episodes in it have urged me (sorely against my will) to let them be printed here; and, perhaps, if they serve as a warning to anyone—if *he* be still in this world—— But I had better tell what I have to tell, and leave you to judge whether I have been wise or not in doing so.

We were staying at a pension kept by a Madame Vambèry, just outside the little town of Abondance, among the Swiss Alps. It was a charming place, a sort of big, rambling châlet, built on the wooded slope of a steep hill, commanding a glorious view of the snowy mountains which framed us in on all sides but one; and looking straight down on the little town, with its picturesque jumble of red roofs and twisted chimneys, and the narrow rock-bound river which girdled its foundations like a dark-blue ribbon spangled with silver, or rushed deep and black under grim old arches which threw back its waters in wreaths of turbid foam.

We were a lively enough party at the châlet, Madame Vambèry being a pleasant woman, and having a knack of getting together young and pleasant inmates. I don't remember all of them, for they went and came; but I can recall a nice little Irish doctor, a handsome High Church clergyman and his sister, who went down regularly every morning to early mass in the town below; a French marquise, middle-aged, but fascinating; a newly-married couple, also French; and Helen Joyce, with whom I was travelling. I was then six-and-twenty, in high health and spirits, and un-married; while she was still wearing her first widow's weeds. Indeed, it was as a help to recovering her spirits, sorely tried by her husband's death, that I had agreed to spend the year which had still to pass before my John would be ready for me in travelling with her.

I only mention this to show how I came to be there. Otherwise, neither my affairs nor Helen's have anything to do with this narrative, or contain the smallest interest for anyone else.

Unquestionably, the most interesting members of our party were the newly-married couple. They were both very young (she could scarcely have been eighteen) deliciously good - looking, over head and ears in love with one another, and had only been married a week! This last fact, from which the previous one naturally resulted, leaked out from the guile-less chatter of the little bride herself, and naturally made them even more the central objects of observation and curiosity than they might otherwise have been; but, indeed, the young wife was pretty and innocent enough to attract notice anywhere—fresh from the convent-school where she had passed all her young life, naïve as a babe and playful as a kitten, with big black eyes, most childishly round and liquid, a little head covered with short soft curls, and a complexion of milk and roses.

The husband, however, was even more remarkable for beauty : tall and slenderly made, with a perfectly oval face, long waving hair of a rich auburn colour, with pointed beard and moustachios slightly deeper in tint, and eyes the like of which I had never seen before ; which were indeed the chief feature in his face, and which, though I could not call them beautiful, as some did, would have marked the man among a hundred others after years of forgetfulness.

If some of you think that this is an after fancy of mine, not existent at the time, but created by later impressions, you are wrong.

What I say of them now I thought then, and even described in a letter which is still extant. 'Eyes not large, but looking so from a singular power of dilation in the pupil produced by any intensity of feeling, pleasant or the reverse; whites very convex, and with the dazzlingly opaque brilliancy of porcelain; iris of a bright golden colour, surrounded by an outer ring of deep greenish gray; the whole shaded, and made additionally noticeable by the straight, sharply-pencilled brows, inky-black, and slightly depressed towards the nose—a peculiarity which became intensified whenever their owner was excited to either irony or vexation, and which lent a curious and, to me, somewhat unpleasant expression to his face.'

The other ladies voted him as handsome as an archangel. Mr. Hume, our clergyman, suggested, half-laughingly, 'A fallen one!' But, whatever our opinions might be, they mattered very little to the subject of them. Those weirdly-brilliant eyes of his, with their orange-tawny light—a light which seemed to come from within, as in those of the leopard and night-hawk—had vision for nothing but the charming face of his young wife, while her innocent gaze seemed to lose itself in wondering admiration as it rested on him.

They were ridiculously in love with one another. We had been talking about the glaciers one day at table d'hôte. He had often been in Switzerland, and was describing some of his feats in Alpine climbing, the while his girl-wife listened delightedly, and now and then put in a whisper to one of us :

'N'est ce pas qu'il est tout à fait montagnard, mon mari?'

Later in the evening, I happened to be out in the garden. It was not a large one, but

had the effect of being so from being laid out
in a succession of terraces cut out of the
steep hillside, and planted thickly with all
manner of flowering shrubs and fragrant,
bright-hued blossoms. Strolling along the
upper of these terraces, I was gazing out
to where the great white mountains showed
forth against a sapphire sky set thick with
golden star-gleams, and inhaling the delicious
fragrance of the pine-woods on the other side
of the little river, when I became aware of
the presence of our young lovers on the path
below me. They were chatting in a little
nook formed by the bench and the angle
of the wall ; he half kneeling on the former,
and supporting her as she sat on the wall, her
little feet crossed and hanging down in front
of her, her slender childish figure pressed
against his shoulder. She had on a black
lace frock, cut so as to leave the neck and
arms bare ; and her pretty shoulders, charm-

ingly white and dimpled, glittered like soft mounds of snow in the moonlight, which poured down on her in a silver rain, touching the little curls on her smooth brow, and turning to frosted bronze the crisp waves of her husband's hair, and the glossy leaves of an oleander, which drooped its rosy-flowered branches above them, and swayed softly in the summer breeze.

'*Eh bien, mon chéri,*' I could hear her saying in her clear little child-voice; 'to-morrow, then, thou wilt take me up to the mountains, and show me where to pick the "edelweiss," to take to my mother when we return ?'

'If we can find a guide,' the husband answered; 'but they say one ought to engage them the day before, there are so many excursionists here at present.'

The little bride pouted, and struck him a playful blow on the mouth with a bunch of heliotrope which she held in one small white hand. The perfume, crushed against his lips, rose up to me in a sweet, sharp puff.

'Guides! What do we want with guides? Have you not told me how well you know these mountains, and how often you have been over them alone? You shall be my guide, Henri. I want no others, *point d'étrangers.*'

'But suppose any accident should happen to you, *petite ange?*'

'Accident! What accident? We are not going up Mont Blanc, and the *pasteur Anglais* takes his sister always with him. *Est-ce que tu me crois poltronne, moi?*'

'*Je te crois tout à fait adorable,*' he answered, and, stooping down, lifted her little sandalled shoe and kissed it. I thought it time to retire, and did so; but there had been no vulgar curiosity in my staying so long.

They did their love-making perfectly openly, and there were several others besides me enjoying the perfumed air on those terraced walks.

Next evening, when we came home from our drive, we found the whole pension in a state of the greatest excitement and confusion. The marquise was in hysterics, Miss Hume's maid crying bitterly in the hall, while madame, pale as death, and with her hair all limp and unfrizzled, was giving distracted orders to half-a-dozen servants at once. She could only answer our questions in incoherent ejaculations.

'The most frightful accident—our dear young *nouveaux mariés.* Alas! that poor man! No, no, it was not *he ;* it was his wife ; that charming, fresh, all-adorable child. She had ventured too near a crevasse to pluck a flower. The piece of snow on which she stood, loosened by the late rains, had slipped and she had fallen. *Dieu nous garde !* it was too horrible to think of. Some one had heard the cries of the poor husband, and had come to the rescue, but it was too late. She was dead—dead! They were bringing her body home now. *Pour son mari ? Hélas !* why ask? They said he had tried to kill himself, too. The guides who lifted her from the crevasse had to restrain him by force from flinging himself in.'

It was too true. We heard it all over again from the Irish doctor, who had started off at once to the scene of the disaster; and I dare say you read it in the *Times* of that week under the head of ' Alpine Accidents,' and with some observations appended to it on the folly of people attempting mountain-climbing without guides.. Indeed, there was nothing else to say. As the paper remarked, such fatalities are only too common, and the sole thing which marked this one as specially sad

was the extreme youth and recent marriage of
the innocent victim.

That same night Miss Hume and I went in
to see the body. It had been laid out in a
lower room, and hearing that the poor child's
mother had been telegraphed for, we had
gathered all the white flowers we could find to
strew round the corpse, and so soften the
sorrowful sight to those to whom it must be
agony to gaze upon it.

It was a far more terrible one to us than we
had expected. Not that there were any
horrible facial wounds or disfigurement.
Curiously enough, as the servants had already
told us, there was not a broken bone or a
bruise on the whole body. Indeed, it must
have been the mere shock of falling from such
a giddy height that killed her, for she was
found quite uninjured outwardly, lying on a
bed of soft snow at the bottom of the crevasse;
but to look on the expression of her young

face one would have thought she had died in the most awful agony, so ghastly was the look frozen there in death——a look, not of pain, but of unutterable, indescribable fear, of frenzied horror and repulsion ; while the tiny waxen hands, which some pious soul had tried to bind together cross-wise on the breast, were bent backwards, with the stiffened fingers curving towards the palm, as though warding off some sudden, unimaginable horror.

Miss Hume could hardly bear the sight. She put her hand over the contorted baby-features, and said faintly :

' Oh, would not one think there was no loving God behind death when a little girl can meet it so !   Fancy a mother having only that look to remember her child's face by ! Has no one a veil to cover it ?'

I said I had, and sending her away, for she was quite unnerved, went to get it.

When I returned I forgot to bring a candle

with me, and found the room in darkness, save
for a broad stripe of moonlight falling through
a window at one end of it upon the bier, which,
with its slender white-robed occupant, stood in
the centre of the floor. As a clergyman's
daughter, and going to be a clergyman's wife,
I had no fear of death, and not thinking that
there was anyone else in the room, I was
going in softly, when I stepped back, shocked
and startled at finding myself in the presence
of the widower. He had not seen me. He
was standing on the further side of the bier,
his tall figure slightly bent over it, his arm
raised high above his head, with the hands
wreathed together and waving to and fro, as
if in utterance of some prayer or malediction
against the woe which had fallen on him;
while, though the spot where he stood was all
the darker for being just outside that one ray
of light, I could see his eyes dilated to double
their usual size, and blazing like two un-

earthly lamps with a ghastly yellow glare, which seemed to positively irradiate the dark and tortured face beneath them.

Fully believing that the man had gone out of his mind with grief, I fled, pale and terrified, to my room, where I found Helen's maid was already packing our things for going. She said that, considering the state of her mistress's health and spirits, she had persuaded her not to remain in a house with death in it so soon after her own sad loss, and that, after some discussion, Helen had agreed to leave on the morrow. I was not sorry to hear it.

CHAPTER II.

THE SECOND TIME.

'WELL, be sure and call me if I can be of any use, Mrs. Critchett.'

' I will, ma'am, thank you; and glad I should be to do so if it were in the night, and the nurse not here. They have engaged one. I made a point of it when I let 'em the rooms; seeing as how that was a thing I could *not* feel called on for, with my other lodgers to see to and all. But from what she says now, I shouldn't be a bit surprised if it was before the time. These young things never do calculate right with their first.'

' Has she no mother, Mrs. Critchett ?'

'She has not, ma'am, which is maybe the reason I feel for her, being young too, as I said, and more ignorant of the world and its wickedness than nine out o' ten gurls nowadays. A most pious and godly young creetur' as ever I see ; an' not over-strong. Sits there doing her bits of sewing for the baby as is coming with her Bible on her knee all day long, and sleeps with it under her piller at night. Even my 'usband, he says it's as good as reading a chapter to hear her talk ; which no offence to you, ma'am, all the same, as of course she is nothing but a Quaker, which nat'rally you, being a clergyman's wife, might objec' to have anythink to do with.'

"I should object to myself very much, Mrs. Critchett, if I had any such feeling, or my husband either ! so don't forget to mention to your young lodger that if she feels nervous or ailing, there is a lady upstairs who will be very glad to come and see her, or to help her in any way.'

It was the winter of 1875. I had been married nearly six years, and John and I were living in lodgings in Guildford Street, Blooms-bury, not far from St. Thomas's Church, where my husband was senior curate. I should have preferred a house of my own ; but circumstances made lodgings more practicable to us just then ; and these were very clean, comfortable ones, and kept by an exceedingly worthy woman. We had the drawing-rooms and the best bed-rooms above ; and besides us there were in the house three other lodgers ; a clerk in some City house and his wife, who occupied the dining-rooms, and a queer old bachelor, who lived in one room at the top of the house, and whom we had never yet seen, though he was an older resident than ourselves, and we had lived with Mrs. Critchett for over three years. As for the couple downstairs, they had only been there for three months; and all I knew of them was that I used to get a glimpse, now and then, of a stoutish, thick-set young man, with light hair and a florid complexion, going in to the City of a morning, also that he and his wife had not been married long, and that she was understood to be in a delicate state of health.

Probably for that reason, she went out very seldom, except after dusk, and leaning on her husband's arm ; and though I had passed her two or three times on the staircase, or at the door of her room, I had no very distinct impression of her, save of a fair, slenderly-made young woman, with a very good, pure-looking face, to which her simple dove-coloured gowns and muslin caps lent a certain soft attractiveness.

My offer to be of any service to her in her trouble, however, had not come a day too soon, for that very night the summons arrived.

About nine o'clock Mrs. Critchett came running to tell me that 'poor Mrs. Jones was took bad. Her husband had gone for the nurse and doctor, and would I mind stepping down and comforting her a bit.' Of course I went. There was not very much for me to do, however, though my inclination to do it was enhanced now that I had time to appreciate more thoroughly the absolute beauty of holiness shining from the pale young face which I found lying so patiently on its pillows below. She was very weak, and suffering a great deal ; but she made no complaint or fuss, and indeed hardly spoke, except to utter a gentle 'Thank you,' now and then ; or a more pathetic, 'Thou art very good to me, friend. It grieves me to trouble thee.' When the doctor arrived, he said all was going on as well as possible ; and, indeed, a very few minutes after Mr. Jones returned with the nurse (who lived at the other side of

London, and had not expected to be wanted so soon) everything was over, and there was another tiny citizen the more in the world.

I had gone back to my own rooms by then, not wishing to be in the way, and thinking that between husband, nurse, doctor, and landlady, those very small apartments downstairs would be sufficiently tenanted. Indeed, I was in the act of telling John, who had just come in, all about it, and what a nice gentle creature the young Quaker wife seemed to be, when the stillness which had followed pleasantly on the late bustle and upset in the house was broken by a sudden hoarse shriek; then an opening and shutting of doors, and the sound of footsteps hurrying to and fro.

'Something is wrong. What can it be, John?' I said, getting up, and looking apprehensively at my husband, and almost in the same moment Mrs. Critchett's maid came to the door with a breathless message:

'Oh, if you please, ma'am, missus says could you come at once. She thinks Mrs. Jones is going.'

'Going!' By the time I had got from my room to hers, it was plain that she was so far gone that the eyes into which mine looked would never know me or any earthly thing again on this side of the grave. In sober truth, I hardly knew her! The apartment had been tidied and put straight. There was a pleasant glow of fire and lamplight in it, the latter carefully shaded from the face which lay back upon its pillows just as I had left it barely an hour ago. But during that short time such a change had come over the features as no mere womanish pain or distress had had power to bring into them previously; and before which all that exquisite, calm trustfulness, which had been their principal characteristic before, was blotted out as completely as though a livid and alien mask had been pressed down

upon them. And such a mask! Such a
ghastly presentment of unutterable woe,
horror, and repulsion — agonized, terror-
stricken repulsion, as I had never, in all my
life, seen on any human face before, *save one!*
The face of that girl-bride who perished in the
Swiss Alps.

I had forgotten her. The whole incident
had slipped from my mind until recalled to it
now, seven years afterwards, by that never-
to-be-forgotten look of mortal, unendurable
terror, repeated even in the very pose of
the poor hands which, damp and clammy
in death's closing grasp, were yet lifted up
with the palm turned outwards and the fingers
slightly curved, as though in a last effort to
thrust from her something, or some vision, too
horrible to see and live.

She was not quite dead, however, though
the only sign of life was a faint convulsive
shivering of the limbs and lips ; and both the

nurse and landlady vied with me in striving,
by applications of ice, brandy, etc., to recall
the fast-ebbing sands of existence, the while
the last-named woman answered as well as
she could my horror-stricken inquiries as to
the cause of the terrible change before me.

'Ma'am, she was going on as well as
possible. Very weak, but nothing in the
world wrong; though the baby, poor thing,
is but a measly bit of a creature, and not like
to live, the doctor says. He had done all as
was needed, and was in a hurry to get off to
another case, so after he'd spoke to Mr. Jones,
and told him he might go in and see his wife
(as was asking for him), off he went. I let
him out myself, and then went into the little
back room there to nurse, who was 'tending
the baby. She told me she'd just shown
the gentleman in here, and bid him be careful
not to excite his good lady; but, indeed,
there seemed no fear of that, for he went in

as soft and quiet as a mouse, while she was lying smiling on her bed like any angel, as calm and still.

' " And an angel she's been all through," I said, when the words were hardly out of my mouth but there came a shriek from this room as you might have heard upstairs, and as hardly sounded like her voice, though we knew it couldn't be no other. Nurse and me we rushed in, and there she was, sitting bolt upright in bed with her arms lifted up and her face like it is now, and him—Mr. Jones, I mean—trying to lie her down and soothe her.

' We put her back almost by force like, for she seemed quite unconscious and stiff, as if she was in a fit; and he began telling us as he'd hardly said a word before a donkey, as was kept in a yard near by, suddenly brayed out loud, and so startled her she sprang up in bed with the scream we heard, when nurse here she stopped him, and bid him run for dear life after the doctor and fetch him back.

' "Never mind what frightened her," said she, " but go this minnit. She's dying now, an' if you don't catch up with him she'll be gone before you get back." '

There was a knock at the door at that instant, and with the exclamation, ' There he is !' Mrs. Critchett broke off in her narrative and hurried out. A second later and we heard her opening the front door, and speaking volubly to someone there ; then steps coming along the corridor, and another voice—a voice that somehow sent a cold, strange thrill through me, though I had no recollection of ever having heard it before—asking in tones which, low as they were, penetrated clearly to where I stood, ' Is she still alive ?'

Someone else heard the question besides me—the dying woman ! I was holding her,

supported on my arm ; and at the first sound
of that voice I felt a sharp, swift shiver run
through her entire frame, while for one instant
the secret horror hidden behind those glazed
and staring eyeballs flashed into sudden life.
The white lips met with a sharp, hissing gasp,
and then dropped apart ; the hands fell
heavily at her side ; the eyelids closed.

She had died—died while her husband was
still asking if she lived.

Involuntarily I sank down upon my knees
and bowed my head upon the bedclothes. At
such a moment—the moment when a soul is
suddenly torn away from earth and set before
the judgment-seat of God—prayer seems the
fittest and only attitude for those called on to
witness the solemn change. Another step
had, however, already entered the room, and
as it slowly advanced to the foot of the bed
I looked up, meaning to say such poor words
of sympathy or comfort as might come to my

lips to aid the man so terribly stricken in the first recognition of his bereavement.

They were never uttered ! Instead, I found myself staggering dumbly to my feet, with eyes fixed and staring, and a sudden icy coldness at my heart, as though every drop of blood there had been jerked violently upwards to my confused and startled brain. Where— where and when had I seen before—not *this* man now facing me, this plain, dull-browed, sandy-haired English clerk, with whose back-view only I had hitherto been familiar—not him ; but *his eyes !* eyes unlike in shape and colour every other feature in his face, dark and sinister, with abnormally dilated pupils, black, sharply-lined brows, with a deep depression towards the centre of the nose, and irides of a lurid orange hue which seemed to glow and scintillate as with some inward flame ?

I have no remembrance of how I left the room.

*   *   *   *   *

Next morning, before I was up, John spoke very seriously to me, warning me never to say to anyone else what I had told him the previous night, and blaming me for letting my imagination (as he called it) affect my nerves and moral judgment in the way it had done. He pointed out to me that sudden death might not unnaturally leave a more painful expression on the face than a gentle or lingering one, and that it was the recollections suddenly recalled to me by this one when I was tired and over-excited, and not any real resemblance, which had induced me to fancy a similarity between the personality of our fellow-lodger and the handsome young Frenchman of seven years back.

He told me also that he had seen the former several times, and could not detect anything weird or unusual in his eyes save that they, as well as the brows, were rather darker than

the general tone of his colouring warranted;
and that from what he heard from the nurse
and doctor, he was of opinion that the poor
young woman's death resulted from perfectly
natural causes, and such as would most probably be induced in a nervous woman in her
condition by any sudden fright or strain to the
system. He said this and a good deal more,
and I listened and was silent. I even tried
to believe that he was right, and did not ask,

'But *was* she a nervous woman, or one
peculiarly the reverse; and why should I, on
whose strength and common-sense you have
relied for six years, and who have stood with
you beside many and many a death-bed, and
helped you to comfort all sorts and conditions
of mourners, turn suddenly, and without any
cause, nervous and fanciful also ?'

That evening Mrs. Critchett came to tell
me that the baby was dead also, and that
the widower had given her notice, saying

that he could not bear to stay in the house
once the double funeral was over. She
added :

'Not that a day-old child can make much
difference to him, poor man ; and, for my
part, I think it's better out of the way. It
was miserably delicate from the first, and had
the queerest eyes, black and uncanny as a
little imp. For that matter there's something about the father's—God forgive me
for saying it of him, poor soul !—which
always make me feel a bit creepy. Did you
ever notice them, ma'am ?'

CHAPTER III.

THE THIRD TIME.

WHAT follows is taken from my last year's note-book, the Christmas week of 1882. I copy it just as it stands, without any alteration whatever, save as regards the actual names of the town and people concerned in it. As I am still living in the former, and my husband is rector of the parish, it might possibly be injurious to him or others were I to omit this one caution.

Nov. 25th.—Just a month to Christmas, our first Christmas at the rectory! What a stately, comfortable sound it has, and how well it suits John ! He seems actually growing stouter to fit it. Martha tells me that the house adjoining ours is let at last. I am glad of it, for it is a serious drawback to our pretty, cheerful home to be obliged to look out on those desolate, weed-grown gardens, those rows of gaunt and shuttered windows. It is a large house too, and one of the oldest in the place. They say one wing dates back nearly two hundred years; but it belongs to a family who do not live there, and it has been unlet for a long time. I believe there is some talk of its being haunted, and that tenants will not stay in it. I hope the new ones will prove exceptions to the rule. It is quite cheering even to see the huge iron gates standing open, and painters and glaziers already hard at work all over the premises.

Nov. 30th.—I have been listening to a terrible story to-day—a ghost story, too, of all things in the world for a sober rector's wife to give ear to; but as it relates to The Priory (the name by which the house adjoining ours is known), and explains the holy horror with which even the schoolchildren regard that mansion, I thought I might be excused for letting the old woman who comes to mend my carpets give me her version of the legend in question. I need hardly say that she believes in it most implicitly herself.

It seems that about a hundred years ago it belonged to a member of the Thorpe family who had made a very unfortunate marriage. That is to say, he had married a very young and lovely girl who had all the outward semblances of purity and innocence, and who, nevertheless, turned out to be as shamelessly wicked as what old Mrs. Luton calls 'the baddest lot in the town.' Not content with being false to her husband, she used his absence in America, on diplo-

matic business connected with our ratification
of the lately-fought-out independence of the
colonies there, to turn the dignified old Priory
into a pandemonium of such reckless license
and dissipation as filled the whole county
with the scandal of the doings there, and
caused her dissolute companions to be
publicly hooted in the streets of the little
township.

It is surmised that she and one of them
had planned an elopement to take place
before the return of the injured husband from
abroad, and so place her in safety from his
wrath; but, if so, her scheme was frustrated.
Major Thorpe returned three weeks sooner.
than had been expected, and was met on
landing by an old servant who had left The
Priory in disgust at the scenes enacted there,
and who lost no time in acquainting his
master with them.

The scene which followed must have been

a terrible one; for even at this distance of
time the old woman's voice sank, and she
looked furtively about her before telling of
it. At first, indeed, Major Thorpe said
nought, but struck down and went nigh to
murder the man who had dared to blacken his
wife's fame to him; but when convinced of
the truth of his story, he lifted his two arms
to heaven and swore so terrible an oath
of vengeance as curdled the very blood of the
listener to hear—offering himself to perish
everlastingly in the nethermost flames of hell
if for those dishonoured seven months of his
absence he might be allowed, not only to
punish her who had polluted them, but once
in seven years to wreak such residue of his
wrongs as her mere death could not atone
for on some other woman, young and pure
and innocent as she had seemed to be,
and so satisfy his tortured soul for the worse
torture that first woman had inflicted on him.

Next day it was rumoured among some in the town that Major Thorpe had been seen in the neighbourhood; and one old gardener even swore to having seen a figure which he recognised as his master's lurking among the shrubs in The Priory garden; but no hint of this reached the guilty revellers within, or perhaps they might even then have escaped the doom hanging over them.

That same night a sudden cry of 'Fire!' was raised in the quiet old town; and folks, roused from their sleep and rushing to the spot, saw flames pouring from the lower windows of that part of The Priory which the frail Mrs. Thorpe inhabited. The servants, who slept in another wing, were already awaked, and had made good their escape; but all their attempts at rescuing their mistress proved futile, the door opening from the great hall to her suite of apartments being found to be locked and barred; while through crack and keyhole poured a crimson glow which showed that all within was already a sea of roaring flame.

And then, while the shrieks of the victims within and the crowd without rent the air, and while some ran for water and some for ladders, and some fled hiding their eyes for very fear and horror, there was seen at one of the upper windows an awful sight; for there, during the space of one minute, there appeared, as if painted against a curtain of lurid red and framed in wreaths of smoke, three figures—a man and woman, and between them Major Thorpe, holding a hand of each clasped together in the iron clutch of one of his, and with the other levelling a pistol menacingly at the head of the man, whose left arm hung, evidently broken, at his side; the while the woman writhed and shrieked and clung to him with vain cries for mercy.

One second, I say, this was visible. The next there came an awful crash, as though a magazine had exploded at their feet, and in a breath the whole front of the house, roof, windows, walls and all, disappeared and crumbled away in a vast sheet of white flame which shot high into the air and sank down, carrying those three figures with it.

No smallest portion of their bodies was found when the ruins came to be searched afterwards; and in course of time the Thorpe family rebuilt the house as it now stands, and announced it as to let; but already an evil name had accrued to it. People spoke of cries issuing from the empty rooms, and of a shadowy male form seen prowling along the galleries of the one wing of the ancient building still remaining, or in the deserted garden; and though tenants came, it was only to go again the more quickly.

It remains to be seen if the new people (an Indian colonel and his wife) will be braver.

But I am half ashamed to have listened to such a farrago of romance and superstition, after all. I hope no one will whisper a word of it to my little Jo. He is fond of making his way into that garden and playing there.

Dec. 15th.—They are come, and I have seen them ; that is, I have had a distant view of them from my bedroom window, as they stood on their lawn together : he, a tall, white-haired, soldierly-looking man, with a long moustache; she, a singularly slender, graceful woman, in black, with a large silver cross round her neck, and seemingly much the younger of the two. People who have met them tell me they are both delightful, and the greatest acquisition to the place that it has had for years; but I fear we are not fated to know much of them. Colonel Thorpe (he is a distant cousin of the owners of the house) is an avowed freethinker, and his beautiful wife —what sounds far worse in the ears of our good townsfolk—a papist! 'A most devout one, too,' Lady Fanshawe, our patron's wife, told me. 'Had set her heart on going into a convent when Colonel Thorpe met her, and fell so in love with her he persuaded her to marry him instead. A sweet creature, with a delicious, nun-like unworldliness added to her new matronhood, which makes me quite in love with her myself. You mustn't call there, however. That bad colonel hates parsons, and swears he won't have anyone from a parson's house inside his. Isn't it dreadful of him?'

'And his wife?' I said.

'Oh, my dear, didn't I tell you she was a Romanist, and you know the ill-feeling here against the late rector for his ritualistic tendencies. It would never do for you or your husband to seem to run after her. Your parishioners would be in arms against you at once.'

What narrow, narrow places provincial towns are !

Dec. 23rd.—Something has happened which has upset me terribly ; I do not know what to think of it, whether I am under a delusion, or am not so strong as I was ; or what it portends, if indeed it portends anything. If John were only here ! But he left yesterday for Dullminster on a visit to the bishop, and will not be back till this afternoon. Perhaps, too, he would only laugh at me. Once before, that time in Bloomsbury, he said it was imagination ; and now—— But I had better write it all down. Perhaps, if it looks ridiculous on paper, I may be able to feel the foolishness of it myself.

I was going down to the church yesterday afternoon to see about the decorations. There

is a narrow lane dividing the Priory grounds
from the churchyard, which makes a short cut
from our house to the latter; and along this
I was hurrying, when, midway in it, I en-
countered Colonel Thorpe.   He was carrying
a leather hand-bag, as if bound on a journey,
and as it was the first time I had had an
opportunity of seeing him close, I naturally
slackened my pace a little, so as to get a better
view of him.   Believe me when I say it, I
had no other thought in my mind, no other
motive than the natural womanly curiosity to
look at one who was not only our nearest
neighbour, but a man of good position in the
county; and my first glance at the tall,
erect figure, the white locks, and long gray
moustache, with pointed military tips, gave me
a distinct feeling of admiration.   In the same
moment, however, I was conscious of a change
coming over me; a kind of coldness, mingled
with a nervous thrill, which quickened as

he grew nearer. Instinctively I hung back, a sort of chilled expectancy, though of what I knew not, clogging my steps; while, by contrary impulse, dread, blended with desire, drew my eyes more and more eagerly to his. A double wave of memory seemed to sweep over me—sharp peaks of dazzling snow rising against a sapphire sky, the scent of heaped white flowers on a silent form; and anon a close sick-room, cold, clutching hands, and the wail of a babe near by. A mist was gathering over my gaze, my hands felt cold, my head giddy; and, instead of the man before me, I seemed to see the outline of a window filled with lurid flame, and gleaming out of it a pair of eyes—fierce, dark, with hugely dilated pupils, and irides of a tawny yellow, glowing like two hellish coals with inward fire; the very eyes—God help me now, as I speak the truth!—which seven years before had met mine over the lifeless body of the

City clerk's young wife; which once again, seven years before that, had lit with such a wild and ghastly glare the dark face of the young Frenchman in the Swiss châlet! And then, in the same moment, the mist cleared, and I saw the eyes only, and knew that they were in Colonel Thorpe's face, and that *they recognised me !*

Aye, believe it or not, they did ; and I knew it ; not by any process which I could describe to you—for, indeed, I am not clever at analyses of any sort—but by that nameless sympathetic flash and thrill, that upleaping something in the gaze, which says to you, and everyone meeting it, whether they can answer it or not, ' I know you !'

There was no syllable spoken, no pause on either side. We met, and passed, and I went on to the church ; but in such a tumult of feeling as I pray God I may never experience again : so shaken, and filled by an overpowering sense of some terrible impending calamity, which, nevertheless, I did not think of as affecting me, as shook me to my very centre with impotent terror and anxiety.

For what could I do, or say, that would not proclaim me a hopeless maniac were I to strive to avert an evil, which even in my madness (if madness it was) I could not dare to put into words, if I could find words to put it in, and which all the time I felt myself hopelessly powerless to avert? How could I call at the Priory, intrude on its stately young mistress, and implore her to fly from her home and seek shelter with a stranger like me, or anyone else, from her own natural protector, the husband for whose love she had given up her own holiest hopes and ambitions? And yet it was over her head I knew the doom to be impending; and, hour by hour, as I sat trying to work or read in my own peaceful house, I felt it coming nearer and nearer to the ill-fated one adjoining us, and saw again the mocking, pitiless gleam of those eyes defying me to war against the lost soul behind them.

And it only wanted two days to Christmas! Everything else looked so gay, so tranquil. I even caught a glimpse of her during the day speaking to a couple of poor tramps at the gate, and bringing them bread and meat in her own hands.

I must hurry on.

When night came I could not sleep. I had felt better and more cheerful during the evening. In fact, I had taken the trouble to ascertain that Colonel Thorpe had really been starting for London when I saw him that afternoon, and would not return till next day. The doom, then, whatever it might be, was not to fall immediately on its innocent victim. Providence might even yet show me some means for warding it off, and directly I felt this my spirits rose, and I even felt able to laugh at myself for my forebodings, and to feel glad John was not at home to scold me for them.

But after I was in bed sleep would not come to me. I was not ill or feverish, my head did not ache. There was nothing the matter with me except that, try as I might, my eyes would not close in slumber. I remained wide awake for a couple of hours or more, and at last, wearied of lying thus, got up and went to the window, meaning to look out at the night before lighting a candle and trying to read myself to sleep.

It was then just on the stroke of one. The whole town was asleep and in bed, and over everything reigned that perfect stillness which in London it is impossible to find at any hour. Opposite me was the Priory, shuttered and silent too, and its gardens white with frost and bathed in the full rays of the moon, save where a belt of trees or shrubbery cast darkly-waving shadows on the silvery surface.

I was still gazing, when suddenly one of these shadows seemed to detach itself from the rest, and glide forward with a motion suggestive of some crouching creature unwilling to be seen. Involuntarily the old woman's story of the Priory ghost flashed back upon my mind, and I leant forward to see better; but in the same moment the moon had passed behind a cloud, and the shade disappeared, sucked back into the general obscurity of the shrubs through which it had seemed to be creeping: only for an instant, however! The next, the full silver orb rode out again calm and bright as ever upon the blue expanse, and as it did so the bushes swayed and parted, and out from among them stepped a tall black figure, which stood erect in the moonbeams—no ghost, but a man, and the man I had thought of as at that moment far and safely away—Colonel Thorpe !

There was no mistaking him; no possibility of delusion. For two full seconds he stood there in the white moonlight, dressed as I had seen him earlier in the day, with his blanched hair and long curved moustache glittering in the silver rays, and then plunged again into the shadow, and disappeared in the direction of the house.

January 30*th*, 1883.—It is many weeks since I have written in my diary. I have been ill for almost the first time in my life— very ill. They would not even let me write letters for some time, but now that I am well and feeling strong again I must add a few words.

I think it was about mid-day on Christmas Eve that the news reached us that young Mrs. Thorpe was dead. The lady's-maid had found her bed unslept in in the morning, and on search being made she was discovered in the library (a room in the older part of the house), on her knees, and stone dead. It seemed that she had told the maid on the previous evening not to wait up for her, as she had promised to do some copying for the Colonel, which might keep her up late ; and from her position, combined with the papers on the table and an overturned chair behind her, it was surmised that she had been suddenly startled from her occupation by some sight or sound—though what, none could say —and had actually died of fright.

Colonel Thorpe was away in London at the time; but by a curious chance had left for home before the telegram summoning him arrived, and he appeared among the bewildered and terrified servants within half an hour of their discovery of his wife's body. One of them told me afterwards it was a sight to make the bravest shudder—he standing there gazing at her as if turned into stone, and she, his wife, stretched at his feet with that awful look of terror—the terror that had killed her—still staring dumbly from her dead face, and the silver cross she generally wore held stiffly up in both the poor cold hands, as if in mute appeal to Heaven.

The husband has gone abroad again now, and the Priory is once more untenanted. They say it will be pulled down, for that after what has happened this time no one will ever live in it again.

*   *   *   *   *

With this fragment from my diary, my story ends. I have nothing more to say, and no arguments to put forward. If, indeed, such a thing be possible as that He who permitted the Evil One to exercise his will on holy Job, and suffered to take place the yet more mysterious temptation of the desert, should, for some unknown dispensation, have allowed the curse of a lost and reckless soul to take actual form and shape, and by the mere revelation for one instant of its infernal personality crush out as instantaneously and irremediably the spark of life in its hapless victims, it is not for me to say; nor is this the place for the discussion of such suggestions. All I wish to repeat, and I do so most earnestly, is that the facts I have narrated did actually take place, and that I, a practical, commonplace, unromantic woman, did actually see and witness them. If to other minds they offer an easy and un-alarming explanation, I am glad of it; but I would rather not discuss it with them. I will only mention that both Miss Hume and the landlady in Guildford Street are anxious to confirm my account of the events relative to the latter's lodgings and the Swiss pension.

NOT EXPLAINED.

NOT EXPLAINED.

PART I.

THE SHADOW IN THE PARK.

ELEVEN years ago it was. Aye, eleven I remember; for it was the year after I got my first picture into the Academy (I had only gone in for Suffolk Street and the Dudley before), and that was in 1877. It was very early in the spring, too, and I was down in Surrey sketching, working up backgrounds, in fact, for a couple of pictures, both of which I hoped soon to submit to the dread conclave who rule the fates at Burlington House. There was a little inn at the meeting of three cross-roads, somewhere between Dorking and Shere; and there I put up for my headquarters, making longer or shorter excursions therefrom according as I found the neighbouring skies and 'bits' propitious or the reverse.

I had been out one day painting at a bit of moorland ; dark-brown earth, dashed here and there with a bit of golden furze-blossom ; two or three tall fir-trees standing up to the right, their trunks picked out sharply against a pale, far-off sky. It was for a background for my 'Priscilla the Puritan Maiden,' the best bit of colouring I ever did. Not that you will remember it, however ; though it wasn't rejected either. I wish it had been, instead of being 'skied' where no one could see it, in the darkest corner of the Academy, and obliged to stick there till the end of July ; when Willis, the picture-dealer, saw it in my studio, and said :

'My dear fellow, if you'd shown me that before you sent it in, I might have offered you three figures for it.'

As it was, he didn't offer me anything ; and

if you want to see it you've only to look under a pile of old canvasses in my models' dressing-room. It would go for under three figures now; but that has nothing to do with my story.

I had been painting for the best part of the day, as I have said, making the most of the sky, a misty opaline tint throwing up the fir-trees wonderfully, and giving an improved tone to the browns and madders of the bit of moorland; and then a sudden breeze sprang up; the sun came out brightly; the dim, pearly sky broke up into sharp whites and blues; and I packed up my traps to go home. The 'effect' was over for that day, at all events, and I wanted a walk. There was a good bit of afternoon still before me. I determined to take a new route homewards, and go through the park of a certain nobleman in the neighbourhood: a place of which I had often heard, though I had never happened to visit it before.

Wonderfully beautiful, too, it was when I got there, which was not for some time, as I didn't know my way a bit, and had an unconquerable dislike (I have it now) to asking it of other people.

The land rose and fell, now in sharp ridges, thickly wooded with deep, ferny clefts between; now in smooth, green rollers, like the waves of an inland sea, dotted over with huge beeches, and set off here and there by a dark Scotch pine, or an emerald larch in all the first glitter of its early spring garniture. It was a lovely scene altogether, and I wandered on, now taking one path, now another; and anon striking across the grass to catch a nearer view of one of the soft-eyed, slim-legged deer, or disturb a hare from its bracken covert.

All at once it occurred to me to wonder where I was going.

I was coming down one of the grassy undulations in the park. The sun was just setting, and the light fell on one side of the tall, straight silver stems of the Scotch firs and larches, leaving the other side, dark, and throwing long lines of black shadow across the copper-coloured leaves which covered the sloping woods below, so that they suggested a musical score with its lines and giant black-stalked crotchets. That wood looked too dense, however, to be a portion of the park; and, if it were not, I had strayed to the extreme farthest point from that which I desired to reach. Still, it was better to ascertain the truth; the sun would be down in a few moments ; and if, as I suspected, that mass of brown foliage was the outskirts of Ditchley Wood, I was a good eight miles from home, and had better give up the thought of walking thither, and betake myself instead to Ditchley village, in the hope of finding some sort of a conveyance.

The ground got steeper, and the grass poorer, as I descended. A thin belt of Scotch firs stood up at the bottom, out of an undergrowth of fern and ragged shrubbery; and when I had passed this I saw that my suspicions were correct. My hand rested on the ancient, moss-grown paling which surrounded the park, while beyond the deep ditch on the farther side stretched a narrow strip of brown, marshy-looking moorland shut in by the aforementioned woods.

The sun had set by now, and there was something dark and threatening about the belt of dusky foliage, and deep impenetrable shadow before me; something unspeakably melancholy in that lonely bit of common, broken only by an occasional hillock, or pool of blackish water throwing back a dull gleam to meet the pale light of the evening sky; something which made me inclined to cling to this rotten park paling as a sign of human habitation and civilization. To reach Ditchley, I must cross that bit of common and the wood beyond; if I followed the paling I must come out—somewhere! I determined to follow the paling.

The light grew fainter and more dusky as I advanced, the landscape blacker and more indistinct. I had often been out at this time before: not unfrequently had only found my way back to my lodgings by the clear light of the moon; but never in all my life had I experienced this unaccountable feeling of nervousness and depression, which positively made me start and shiver at the mere sound of a rustling among the firs and undergrowth on my right.

It was nothing but just such a rustling as had several times before disturbed me—the passage of a fallow-deer through the dry fronds of its bracken cover; yet (mock at me if you will) I declare to Heaven I stood still,

drenched from head to foot with a cold dew
of perspiration, and turned my head to look
for the innocent cause of the noise with the
slow, stiff movement of one who expects to
see something terrible—even, perhaps, the
enemy of mankind himself!

Instead, I saw *nothing!* Nothing, that is,
but a darkish patch among the bushes, which
at first I thought was the shadow of a man.
They were not high enough, however, to conceal even a deer ; and the belt of trees among
which they grew was so thin I could clearly
see through it to the steep, grassy ridge
beyond. It could but have been a hare,
startled from its form, and gone before I
could turn my head. I laughed aloud at myself as I walked on ; and then stopped short,
with a positively sick feeling of dread as the
rustling began again ; and this time so like—
to my sharpened senses—the stealthy tread of
a man's footsteps through the brake at my right

hand, that I looked over my shoulder with the full anticipation of seeing him there.

Again—*nothing!* Nothing but a waving shadow among the shrubs, probably cast by one of the fir-trees, and looking blacker for the paleness of the evening light—a mere shade, which might even have been fancy, for it seemed to fade and disappear as I looked at it, and I went on again resolutely. The rustling sound went on too. Yes; there was no mistaking it now. It was the creeping, careful step of a man following something—a man who did not wish to be heard. Could it be—such mistakes have been made through the medium of disordered nerves— the sound of my own footsteps, translated by a feverish imagination to a little distance from me ?

I stood still again to try.

The shadow-tread went on, crushing the dry leaves beneath it step by step; came up to me, still on my right; passed me (it may have been fancy, but I could almost swear I felt the shadow on me then, and with it a strange, cold sensation, as of an icy draught); went on a few yards, and then paused, as though he (if it were a man) had suddenly caught sight of the object he was pursuing.

Quite involuntarily I stepped forward, gazing eagerly to see it too; and, to my great relief, saw, at the distance of about twenty yards from me, a young lady!

The path I was following had been trending upwards for some time. It reached the brow of a long ridge at a little distance, where the slender, scanty-leaved boughs of a tall birch-tree feathered down to near the palings in a sort of natural arch, beyond which you could see a space of cold, gray-blue sky. Beneath this arch she stood, her head turned, looking back over her shoulder at me. She had on a canary-coloured gown, with a white bloominess on the edges of it, as though it were made of velvet, and cut in a quaint, old-fashioned style which we rarely see nowadays except in pictures; the sleeves were puffed, and slashed in some darker colour, above the elbow, and the neck hidden by a ruffling, or kerchief, of lace. Standing there, she looked rather above the middle height in women; and the exquisite shape of her head and limbs—the latter rather expressed than hidden by the straight, clinging folds of her gown; the former uncovered, save for a wreath of soft, shining black hair, curling low on the forehead and down her neck—would have attracted the eye of any man, had he an artist's soul behind it or not. In her left hand she held something like a leathern strap, coiled up; and, as she turned her head, I caught the broken, quivering gleam of what looked like a cluster of diamonds,

pendent from her throat and ears. Her face I
will not attempt to describe. It was simply that
of the most lovely woman I have ever yet seen.

I have said that she was looking back
at me; but as I gazed at her, I saw, with
a return of the same strange feeling I have
before noticed, that her eyes rested, not on
me, but on something to my right, and in the
same moment I felt that she, too, was listening to the shadow. Nay, more; she was
looking at it!

Almost before I could realize all this, the
lovely, listening expression of her face
changed to one of mingled fear and annoy-
ance, struggling with strong, distasteful pride.
She flung back her head with an impatient
gesture, and, turning abruptly round, disappeared over the ridge.

In the same breath the rustling sound
began again, glided from me up the hill,
and disappeared too.

I suppose I must have stood where I was for a minute or so, before pursuing my onward way, in the hope of seeing something more of the lovely lady of the park. I was struggling with my own insane folly in having allowed myself to connect her, even for a second, with the rustling which had disturbed my morbid nervousness, and in having become possessed with the idea that it was she, and no other, whom this creeping shadow was following, and that she knew it as well as I did. I put the fanciful notion from me with an effort, and was trudging slowly on, when a sudden, sharp, wailing cry rose from the other side of the ridge; a woman's cry, so plaintive, so shrill with pain or terror, that, grasping my stick tighter, I tore up the path and gained the spot where the girl had stood, before another minute could have elapsed. The echoes of the cry were still trembling on the air as I stood

there; and I looked down for the cause of it,
fully expecting to see that she had either
fallen, or had been attacked by some animal
which had alarmed her.

To my intense astonishment there was no
one whatever in sight!

The path sloped downwards from my feet,
and stretched out straight and unbroken, with
the high paling and flat common on one side,
and the line of trees at the other.   Just at
the bottom two or three rabbits had come out,
and were feeding at the edge of the grass as
quietly as though nothing had passed that way
within an hour.   They threw back their ears,
cocked up their little white tails, and were off
like a shot when I shouted out:

'Where are you?   Are you hurt?'

But there was no other response, no other
sign of anyone hearing me, and my voice
died away in echoes against the silent woods.
Even the rustling sound had ceased, and with

it the chilly, nervous feeling I had experienced. As I went on, indeed, I began to ask myself whether I had not fancied the cry. I felt as if I had been in a dream, of which the only real thing was the girl I had seen. Probably she was one of Lord Marloes' daughters. There might be a fancy ball that night at the Abbey, and she had dressed early, and come out for a stroll in the park, until disturbed by the intrusion of a stranger like myself. The cry (if cry there had been) had come from the other side of the ridge, and from no great distance; and as the trees were nowhere so thick that I could not see through them for several hundred yards, it was evident that she had neither been hurt nor frightened so seriously as to be prevented from running very swiftly out of sight.

I went on therefore without more delay, and in another minute or two came on a park-keeper's lodge, at a turn in the path,

with a woman sitting outside it peeling
potatoes into a wooden tub.

She stopped to look at me as I came up,
and answered my query as to the nearest
village by pointing smilingly to sundry
columns of smoke rising above the edge of
the common at a little distance, and telling
me that that was Ditchley. Yes, it belonged,
like the Abbey, to Lord Marloes. Married?
Oh, certainly! but a young man with no
daughters, and his wife not to say handsome
anyway; though a dear, good lady, and a
sad invalid. They were having some grand
doings at the Abbey that evening, and my
lord's sister had just called in passing, and
carried off the eldest boy to help with the
decorations in the music-room. She were
handsome, if I liked—a real beauty, with the
true family hair, black as my boot, and blue
eyes; but as to her dress, the dame hadn't
seen her—had been busy indoors, and the

boy had only run in to tell her he was wanted. She didn't know what a fancy ball was—had never heard of it; and as to a shriek (here she stared at me rather sharply, as though thinking I was a little out of my mind), there hadn't been none in her hearing, wi'out I meant the peacocks. My lord kept a ' mort ' of them wild in the preserves; and, indeed, she'd got so used to their screeching that she didn't pay no count to it now.

And that was it, of course! I had not known of the peacocks, or I should not have asked the question; and, for the rest, my last conjecture was probably correct. I don't remember ever laughing more heartily than I did at the recollection of my own fanciful cowardice, when, ten minutes later, I found myself sitting by a blazing fire in the most comfortable room of the Ditchley Arms. I should have liked to have seen my lord's sister again though. The lovely face dwelt in my mind for some weeks; and I even fixed it there by making a sketch of her, from memory, as she stood under the silver birch, looking back at me.

PART II.

LADY DORATHEA.

TEN years had passed over my head since the occurrence of the incident mentioned in my last chapter; and, to speak the truth, it had faded so entirely out of my mind that if anybody had asked me about the events of that spring excursion, I am certain it would not have recurred to my memory as forming one of them.

I had travelled much in the interval; had lived for some time in Rome and Naples; made a name as a successful artist; last, not least, had married and established myself in London, the father of twin girls and a boy—

a man tolerably well-to-do in the world, who papered his house with dingy green, and hung it with cracked Japanese plates made a fortnight back in England. Could any individual have passed more completely out of the realms of youthful dreams and fancies to the modern shams and fashions of the day ?

Among my acquaintances—and being well off, I had a large circle of them—was a Captain Verschoyle, the son of one of our merchant princes, and heir to a collection of pictures worth some hundreds of thousands.

He had a very fair taste for art himself, had had a couple of studies from me ; and had got into a way of dropping in at our house, now and then of an evening, to have a game of billiards with me, or to play over some of his own musical compositions to my wife.

When the time for the annual summer exodus drew near in this particular year, I happened to mention one day that, after a month at the seaside, I was going to take my wife and the children to Reigate for September. Verschoyle was present at the time, and turned round to express his delight. He was going for a fortnight's shooting to a friend's place, about ten miles from Reigate. If we were there, he should be able to see something of us. How jolly!

Of course I echoed his pleasure. The young fellow was a puppy and a noodle; but a gentlemanly puppy too, and not a bad-hearted noodle. I rather liked him on the whole.

Sure enough, I had not been ten days at Reigate, and was standing with a friend one afternoon on the platform of the London and Brighton Station, waiting for the train which was to convey him to town, when, lowering my eyes from one of the most glorious golden sunsets ever vouchsafed to the eye of man, I saw standing up black against the saffron-coloured sky two men at the farther end of the platform, one of whom was making vehement gestures of recognition in my direction.

Needless to say it was Verschoyle, and the next moment we were shaking hands, and he had introduced his friend, who turned out to be his then host, and who met me very cordially, and gave me his card with a hearty invitation to come over to lunch any day and see the picture-gallery, of which he said his brother, the owner of the place, was very proud. When they were gone I looked at the card, and saw written in pencil, under the name and London address, 'Ditchley Abbey.'

Ditchley Abbey! Well! what was there in the name to make me start! I had probably heard of the place before. It was a tolerably well-known one, and belonging to an equally well-known peer. I saw his name in the papers every day. The glories of the Abbey were mentioned with honour in the county guide-book. I had even a dim notion that I had once been to the place, and had seen one of the ladies of the house. It must have been a long time back, at all events. My ideas on the subject were most indistinct; and I had not even had an idea that the Abbey was within a drive of my present residence. My friend's train came up while I was still looking at the card, and I dropped it on the platform, and with it the memory I had been trying to recall.

In due time, however, I drove over to the Abbey, a magnificent place, palatial in size and ugliness, and approached by one of the finest avenues in the South of England; and was welcomed very cordially by my host, who introduced me to his wife and sister-in-law, and a couple of men friends, who, like

Verschoyle, were down for the shooting, and with whom we all sat down to lunch.

During the meal I gathered that Lord Marloes himself was travelling on the Continent for his wife's health; and that his brother was only staying at the Abbey for the home shooting, and the vicinity to the regiment to which he, as well as Verschoyle and one of the other men, belonged.

The conversation, however, chiefly turned on art—in compliment to me, I suppose, as a stranger, and to the idea (only too correct a one, I fear) that painters and singers are never thoroughly happy on any subject out of their own profession. At any rate the usual well-bred sillinesses and inanities common to those cultivated members of society who wouldn't know a Titian from a Gainsborough, if left to themselves, were said by my pretty hostess and her husband, Verschoyle chiming in with the air of an A.R.A. at the very least; and bringing out such a *répertoire* of studio slang in the way of ' bits,' ' effects,' ' modelling,' and ' tone,' etc., that he was equal to a whole crew of second-rate Suffolk Street artists rolled into one; and as soon as lunch was over we repaired to the picture-gallery.

I have no space or time for dwelling on the paintings. There were some very good ones, and some equally trashy; a very fair collection of old masters; and a lengthy array of family portraits. These had a gallery to themselves leading out of the organ-room, and we came to them at the last, our host showing considerably more interest in descanting on them than on the more interesting pictures we had just been seeing.

All at once a strange feeling came over me. I saw nothing, and heard nothing; but my hands grew cold as ice, and a sick, shivering sensation crept along every vein in my body, bringing back to me in one breath the rustling sound of that shadow-step which I had heard, or had fancied I heard, ten years ago, in the very park on to which the windows of the picture-gallery were looking. How it came, or whence it came, I know not ; but in that moment the terror I had so long forgotten was there, as plainly and vividly as though the sound of the stealthy footsteps were even then in my ears. I was standing facing the window, and with my back to a picture. Something made me turn round, though with a feeling of reluctance which I could not define, and look at it. It was the life-size, half-length portrait of a man, in the dress of the Stuart era, very well painted, but with a dark, evil face, strongly lined, and wearing a peculiar look in the eyes, half sombre, half passionate, which gave a sinister expression to the whole countenance.

I had never seen the picture or any copy

of it before. I had never met anyone in the
least reminding me of it. If you ask me
how a face, thus utterly strange and un-
familiar, could remind me of a *sound*, un-
connected with face or shape of any sort, I
cannot answer. I can only aver as solemnly
as I stand here that it did, and so intimately
that one seemed as it were only a con-
comitant of the other. I made no comment
on it whatever. I went on, answered some
queries of my host's relative to another portrait, and then—stopped short, as if struck
by a sudden blow, and cried out so loud as to
startle them all :

' Good Heavens ! I was right. Here
she is too !'

We had come to a long narrow picture,
almost hidden by a projecting pillar at a
corner of the gallery—the portrait of a lady
in a canary-coloured gown, the sleeves puffed
and slashed with dark red, the bodice cut

square over the bosom, whose downy whiteness was partly hidden by a lace kerchief.
Clusters of diamonds and rubies glittered at
her throat, and in her ears; and one hand
was curled round the neck of a huge hound,
whose dark muzzle rested on her knee. Her
hair, which was black and curly, was worn
low on her forehead and down her neck
behind; and the whole face was lit up by an
expression of mirthful sweetness mingled
with an innocent consciousness of her own
beauty. A beautiful face indeed! so beautiful that I had never seen its like but once
before—the face of 'my lord's sister' as
she looked that evening when I met her in
the park.

Naturally my violent start and exclamation
—for which, indeed, I could have bitten out
my tongue—excited no little wonder in those
about me, and my host repeated:

'*She?*   Why, Mr. Le Fane, what can you

know of this too fair and foolish ancestress of mine ?'

The tone was a little haughty, and I stammered something about having taken the face for the portrait of someone else—someone I had seen. I even asked whether it had ever been engraved or exhibited : at a loan-collection perhaps ?

'Oh dear no!' he said. None of the portraits had ever been allowed to be copied or removed from the Abbey; and indeed, till within the last hundred years, this one had not been visible to visitors, being covered with a curtain; and he pointed to some blackened fragments of drapery still suspended to a cord some inches above the frame.

'The portrait, then, has a history?' I said, with as much coolness as I could command. 'Certainly, the original must have been beautiful enough to warrant

one.   May we hear it, if the request is not
impertinent ?'

'By all means.   The fair Lady Dorothea
lived too long ago for her follies to affect us
personally (even as a warning to you, my
dear),' nodding his head at his blooming
sister-in-law, who was somehow always to be
found lingering with Verschoyle in the rear of
the rest of the party.   'The story is only
too common, I'm afraid, and is simply this.
She was very lovely, as you see, and had a
host of lovers, as you may infer.   Also she
was a coquette, and so hard to please that
she couldn't make up her mind as to whom
to take; and a story got about that she had
so far disgraced herself as to set her affections
on a person far beneath her in station—a
groom, I believe, who was, in point of fact,
dismissed his place as soon as the report
reached the ears of the family.   A fortnight
later my lady disappeared too.   She had

been sitting for her picture—you will see that parts of the background and the drapery are still unfinished—and went out into the park afterwards, under pretence of looking for her favourite hound, which, she said, had run away from her. At any rate, she had the leash for his neck in her hand when she was last seen leaving the garden-door, and she returned no more. Every search and inquiry after her was made, headed by her cousin, the bearded gentleman there, at whose portrait you were gazing so intently a few minutes back, and who was one of her most ardent suitors. From private information, however, he learnt in the course of a few days that she had actually fled across the seas with this very servant fellow; and from that day, as you may guess, her name was dropped at the Abbey. The shock and disgrace broke her father's heart. He grew quite childish, shut himself up in his private rooms and would see no one; had that picture, unfinished as it was, hung up in the corner and covered with a black cloth; and died in the course of a year or so.'

'And the cousin?' I asked. It had come over me with an unpleasant thrill that the man with the sinister eyes should, after all, be connected with her.

'Ah! poor fellow, I'm afraid he must have been harder hit by the pretty runaway than men are nowadays. They say he never got over her flight, but moped about for some weeks, and then went away, and joined the Commonwealth in a fit of spleen. At her father's death he became ninth baron, and married a Scotch lady; but the Restoration took place shortly afterwards, and he was of course a disgraced man; and whether it was that, or domestic jars (for they say he led a cat-and-dog life with his wife), or the old wound, I know not, but he died one day by

his own hand. Yes, it is a handsome portrait ; but we are not proud of the original ;
for she was the only woman of our race who
ever " went wrong," as the saying is ; and,
besides, she carried off with her certain things
of great value to the rest of the family.'

'Ah ! the jewels,' said his wife. 'I have
often read of them in the Abbey chronicles.
Have you noticed how beautiful they are in
the picture, Mr. Le Fane ?'

'Yes,' added my host. 'They were given
us by a French king, and were of great value.
She wore them when sitting for her portrait ;
and she ran away with them the same day.
It was unfair of the jade, for they didn't
belong to her, and were doubtless broken up
and sold for a tenth of their value by Master
Groom.'

'But they have been recovered since ?' I
exclaimed. 'The present lord's sister has
worn them, has she not ? Pardon me, I have

an object in asking,' for I saw astonishment on more than one face, and felt that I was bound to explain.

'Most certainly not. They have never even been heard of since her disappearance; nor have we any like them in the family,' said my host. 'May I ask your object in——'

'One moment. You will laugh at me; but let me ask you one other question first. You have or had, ten years ago, a sister, most wonderfully like her ill-fated ancestress, had you not? and who wore a dress, made in exact imitation of this, at an entertainment here? Perhaps you would not know it; but it was in the spring of 1878.'

'Your questions certainly rouse my curiosity for their explanation,' my host answered rather coldly. 'As it happens, however, they are easily answered. We have a sister, undoubtedly, but she does not in any way resemble this portrait. I myself was staying here through the spring and winter of 1878, and, therefore, happen to know that there were no entertainments given here, beyond dinner-parties and one concert, at all. I remember the concert, because my sister came up to arrange about it. It was at the beginning of March———'

'Yes, yes,' I said eagerly; 'the first week.'

'And she took the whole management of it. My brother's wife was then too delicate for anything of the sort. As to her dress, I don't remember what it was—possibly velvet; she is the eldest of the family, you know—but certainly in no way resembling this. Verschoyle knows her very well. She married Lord Castlegarden the year afterwards.'

Lady Castlegarden ! Of course I knew her well, too, by sight; had seen her scores of times in the Park and Row. A handsome

woman enough, but one who must have been
past thirty ten years ago ; a woman no more
like — no more to be compared with the
lovely, liquid-eyed beauty of that spring evening than night is with morning.

In a few words I told them the brief story
of my adventure, and shortly afterwards I
went away.   There had been a great deal of
laughter and questioning, and many exclama-
tions and suggestions that I had seen the
picture, or even a sketch of it, before—perhaps
as a child ; or had heard it described, and
dreamt about it ; or had seen a fancy dress
somewhat resembling the one in the portrait,
and had fancied the likeness in the face. Very
plausible and well-sounding suggestions they
all were ; but, as it happened, in no way
corresponding to the plain, unintelligible facts
of the case, and only affecting me in so far as
to make me glad that there was one point in
the story which I had kept back from them,

as too fanciful even to bear the test of my own repeating—the shadow-step at my side, and the ghastly, unaccountable thrill with which I had connected that step with the sinister-eyed cousin, who, I now learnt, had been one of the Lady Dorothea's slighted adorers.

PART III.

A WITNESS FROM THE DEAD.

As may be easily supposed, after my visit to the Abbey and the story I had heard in the picture-gallery there, the subject of that early adventure with which it had been so strangely connected did not pass out of my mind as rapidly as it had previously done. On the contrary, the laughter and incredulity with which it had been met had exactly the opposite effect. It stimulated me (as soon as I returned to town) to a search among some old boxes containing various 'reliquæ' of my bachelorhood, for the sketch of which I have already spoken, and which I could not remember having destroyed.

If I had ever had any doubts as to the exactness of my own memory, they disappeared at once and for ever when I came, as by a lucky chance I did, upon the missing canvas. With the single exception of the surroundings, my sketch of ten years back might have been one taken from the portrait itself of the lovely Lady Dorothea Dysart then hanging in the picture-gallery at Ditchley Abbey.

Nay, more! The thing 'like a strap,' which I had noticed she held in her hand, I now recognised as the leash for her hound with which, according to the old chronicle, she had gone out on the unhappy day of her elopement. I think I should have written to Verschoyle and mentioned the fact to him, but for an event which drove it out of my mind.

One of my children was taken ill with a dangerous and infectious disorder, and during the long weeks of her malady——a malady to which only death brought a termination——all idea or remembrance of anything connected with the realms of romance was banished from me by the obliterating hand of stern, hourly trouble and anxiety.

You may guess, then, at my surprise, when, about a twelvemonth afterwards, I received a note from Verschoyle, couched in the following words :

' DEAR LE FANE,

    ' Something has been discovered here, strangely connected with that picture in the gallery. It seems to make a horrible sequel to your adventure, of which I'm afraid we made too merry last year. Lord Marloes thinks so, at any rate, and would therefore like you, if you are still interested in the subject, to run down here and see the thing which was found two days ago.

'Yours, etc.,

'E. Verschoyle.

'P.S.—I don't know if you have heard that Tom Dysart has got his majority, and I am engaged to his sister-in-law, the young lady you met here at lunch?'

I had not heard it. I had heard nothing of any of the party since I returned to London, and did not even know that Verschoyle was again at the Abbey. I had missed him from town, but supposed he was somewhere with his regiment, and had not, indeed, given much thought to him. The body of the letter, however, was too mysteriously exciting to be disregarded. Artists are proverbially birds on the wing; and, having previously telegraphed to say I would come, I took the train for Ditchley that same afternoon.

At the Abbey I was received, not by my former host, but by Verschoyle and Lord Marloes himself, the latter of whom met me in the hall with an air of satisfaction at my coming, mingled with a certain gravity and excitement, which showed me that the discovery alluded to was not without serious import. My questions as to what it was were, however, disregarded by both gentlemen; and while I was taking some refreshment after my journey, Verschoyle seized the opportunity to question me over again as to my adventure, which he had already related to Lord Marloes, asking me to repeat every little detail of the walk; and remarking, with some acumen, that my remembrance of the whole affair was more vivid than when I had first spoken of it.

I said that was perfectly true; as, when a long bygone history is suddenly recalled to one's mind, the minor incidents connected with it are less apt to come to the surface, than when subsequent thought has cleared and revivified the impressions of the past. Likewise, that I had been fortunate in finding a sketch made the day after the occurrence I had described; and also some private notes, chiefly relating to sky tints and other data of the day's work, but containing sundry details bearing on the event in question, and which I might otherwise have forgotten.

'A sketch? That is more fortunate than I expected,' cried Lord Marloes. 'You didn't know of that, Verschoyle. I hope, Mr. Le Fane, you have got it with you?'

My answer was to take the canvas from a small square parcel which I had brought into the room, and to lay it on the table before him.

It is unnecessary to dwell on the surprise of both Lord Marloes and his friend when they looked at what was, to all appearance, a copy of the picture upstairs. It was not till after some minutes had been given to its expression, and Verschoyle had pointed out the words, 'A sister of Lord Marloes, taken in Ditchley Park,' with the date roughly scrawled in paint on the back of the canvas, that my host said :

'You mentioned a look of fright and offence on the girl's face; but here it is bright enough, with somewhat of a listening expression, according to my idea.'

'Your idea is correct. That is precisely the expression she wore when she turned her head as if to see whence the approaching footsteps came. It was not till she saw— not till afterwards, that her face changed, and she turned her head directly and hurried on.'

My host looked at me keenly.

'Pardon me,' he said, 'but you altered your sentence just now. You were going to say she saw—what ? May I ask you to go on ?'

'I would rather not, my lord ; simply because what I was going to add appears even to myself too fanciful to be put into words. But it is this. I mentioned to you the rustling sound like the stealthy step of someone following me which first attracted my attention. Well, no sooner did I see the young lady I have sketched, than I became conscious in some unaccountable fashion that it was she, not I, who was being followed ; that she *saw* what I could not see ; and that it was this sight which brought the change over her face which I have described.'

'And you have no idea what it was ? You saw nothing ? You have nothing more to tell us, then ?' cried Lord Marloes, in such evident disappointment, that, at the risk of mockery, I made up my mind to tell him all.

'I saw nothing,' I answered; 'but as to any idea of what it was—if, as I expect, you have already set me down as a maniac, you will not be surprised at what I am now going to tell you being in keeping with the rest of my mania. You know that portrait of this fair lady's cousin? When I came in front of it last year—never having seen it before, mark you! nor having as yet seen hers—I felt (how or why I cannot tell you) that it was the step of the man painted there that I had heard in this park ten years before; and I knew (how or why I cannot tell either) that it was he, and no other, who forced from her that cry for help which had made me hasten, though all in vain, to the rescue.'

My host rose to his feet.

'Whether you are a maniac or not,' he said gravely, 'your story is the strangest and most unaccountable I have ever heard; and you will not think it less so, when you have seen what I have to show you. Will you come this way ?'

Without another word he opened the door and passed out of the room, Verschoyle and I following him.

At the entrance of the picture-gallery, however, those two drew back, and suffered me to precede them a little. I did not go very far !

There, on the wall before me, hung the painted image of the fair Lady Dorothea, whose disgraced name had been a shame and a slur on the family for so many generations, whose bright eyes and laughing lips, which had carried away so many hearts, still beamed on me from the canvas in all the joyous coquetry of her youth and innocence.

There, on the floor beneath it, stood a long deal case, of that ominous shape we all know too well, painted black, and covered with a cloth. At a sign from Lord Marloes,

Verschoyle removed the latter, and, coming nearer, I saw laid within it the fleshless skeleton of a human figure. Brown, bare, hideous and earthy, it lay there, with no sign of womanliness—no trace of beauty left, but with the lambent flash and lustre of the French king's diamonds still gleaming from the flesh-less joints of the throat—still lying on either side of the grisly, blackened skull.

The pictured woman smiled down on me from above; the dead woman grinned up at me from below; and only those jewels re-mained to tell us, who looked upon them, that they were one and the same!

'My God!' I cried. 'Do you mean to say that her body has been found? Where?'

Someone answered; who, I do not know:

'Within a few yards of the path at the farther side of the little hill from which you heard her cry for help.'

'She never eloped then, at all!' I went on,

the ghastly truth dawning more fully on me. 'She was murdered! Good Heavens! murdered, and—not for gain!'

Again someone answered:

'She was murdered, and not for gain. The proof is in those jewels left on her body. Something else was left, too. See!'

It was my host who pointed; and, stooping, I saw what had escaped my eyes before —the handle and a couple of inches of the blade of a short hunting-knife. The remainder of it was buried between the ribs on the left side of the body, where it had been left sticking after the blow was dealt which, in one deep rent, let out the young life within, and made one Cain the more on earth.

'Look narrowly at the handle,' said Lord Marloes, his voice seeming to break harshly on the silence, as we stood gazing downwards, too awed for words. 'You see that it is of silver, and rather curiously shaped;

also, that it bears the family crest.   Now, look there !'

I knew beforehand where he was pointing —at that portrait to which now, as before, I felt an instinctive repugnance to lift my eyes. I knew beforehand that the man there wore a knife with such a handle in his belt.   Not that I remembered having noticed it previously.   Probably most men carried weapons at that time.

'I believe, if one were to take it out and clean it, it would be found to be identical with that in the painting,' said Verschoyle curiously.   No one touched it, however, and as if by one accord we turned shivering away. Somebody lingered to throw the cover again over that ghastly form.   Her name had suffered outrage enough in all these years. It was time to show her some respect now.

Downstairs, Lord Marloes said :

'It was in making a path across the plantation that the labourers came on it, buried in a hollow long overgrown with weeds and brambles. The body had evidently been flung down there immediately after the murder, and loosely heaped over with leaves, boughs and shingle. Time has done the rest. The only wonder is that it was never discovered before.'

'Yes, that is the wonder.' No one said any more. The awfulness and mystery were still too heavy on us. After a minute, Lord Marloes added :

'The knife might have had a fellow, or have been stolen by someone else. We haven't any proof that *he* used it.'

There was no answer this time. I don't suppose that one of us felt the smallest doubt on that subject. If that vision from the dead were not proof, if that nameless thrill creeping over a stranger at the sight of the murderer's face were not substantiation damnable and sure, what evidence could any mortal man bring now to bear upon the past?

I have nothing more to add. I left the Abbey that evening; and I have not happened to meet any of its occupants since. I cannot say I ever wish to enter it again, or that I envy the future wearers of those famous jewels which, for near three hundred years, had been the funeral tiring of a corpse, and are now, I hear, restored to their old dignity in the family coffers.

It is possible that you who read this may laugh at the whole story, and look on me as a lunatic, a spiritualist, or worse. Be it so. All I have to say is this, that which I saw, I saw with my own eyes; that which I did not understand I have not attempted to explain. As to any solution of the mystery, any reason why a stranger and a passer-by should (if it were so) have been singled out for the witness of a message from the grave—a message which yet told him nothing for so many years —those may seek for it who like. For myself, I am not one who shares in the rage for translating everything, no matter how far it is beyond us, to the level of our present stage of small and partially-developed reasoning. Call it the hallucination of a diseased brain, or what you will, the facts are there unalterable; and such as they are, I have given them to you.

DOG OR DEMON?

'DOG OR DEMON?'

'THE following pages came into my hands shortly after the writer's death. He was a brother officer of my own, had served under me with distinction in the last Afghan campaign, and was a young man of great spirit and promise. He left the army on the occasion of his marriage with a very beautiful girl, the daughter of a Leicestershire baronet; and I partially lost sight of him for some little time afterwards. I can, however, vouch for the accuracy of the principal facts herein narrated, and of the story generally; the sad fate of the family having made a profound impression, not only in the district in Ireland where the tragedy occurred, but throughout the country.

' (Signed) WILLIAM J. PORLOCK,

' Lieut.-Col., —— Regt.

' *The Curragh, Co. Kildare.*'

*   *   *   *   *

At last she is dead!

It came to an end to-day : all that long agony, those heartrending cries and moans, the terrified shuddering of that poor, wasted body, the fixed and maddened glare, more awful for its very unconsciousness. Only this very day they faded out and died away one by one, as death crept at last up the tortured and emaciated limbs, and I stood over my wife's body, and tried to thank God for both our sakes that it was all over.

And yet it was I who had done it. I who killed her—not meaningly or of intent (I will swear that), not even so that the laws of this earth can punish me ; but, truly, wilfully all the same ; of my own brutal, thoughtless selfishness. I put it all down in my diary at the time. I tear out the pages that refer to it now, and insert them here, that when those few friends who still care for me hear of the end they may know how it came about.

June 10*th*, 1878. *Castle Kilmoyle, Kerry.*—. Arrived here to-day with K. after a hard battle to get away from Lily, who couldn't bear my going, and tried all manner of arguments to keep me from leaving her.

' What have *you* to do with Lord Kilmoyle's tenants ?' she would keep on asking. ' They owe no rent to you. Oh, Harry, do let them alone and stay here. If you go with him you'll be sure to come in for some of the ill-feeling that already exists against himself; and I shall be so miserably anxious all the time. Pray don't go.'

I told her, however, that I must ; first,

because I had promised, and men don't like
to go back from their word without any cause;
and secondly, because Kilmoyle would be
desperately offended with me if I did. The
fact is, I hadn't seen him for three years till
we met at that tennis-party at the Fitz
Herberts' last week; and when he asked me if
I would like to run over for a week's fishing
at his place in Ireland, and help him to
enforce the eviction of a tenant who declined
either to pay for the house he lived in or leave
it, I accepted with effusion. It would be a
spree. I had nothing to do, and I really
wanted a little change and waking up. As for
Lily, her condition naturally makes her rather
nervous and fanciful at present, and to have
me dancing attendance on her does her more
harm than good. I told her so, and asked
her, with half a dozen kisses, if she'd like to
tie me to her apron-string altogether. She
burst out crying, and said she would ! There

is no use in reasoning with the dear little girl at present. She is better with her sisters.

June 12*th.*—We have begun the campaign by giving the tenant twenty-four hours' notice to pay or quit. Kilmoyle and I rode down with the bailiff to the cottage, a well-built stone one in the loveliest glen ever dreamt of out of fairyland, to see it served ourselves. The door was shut and barred, and as no answer save a fierce barking from within responded to our knocks, we were beginning to think that the tenant had saved us the trouble of evicting him by decamping of his own accord, when, on crossing round to the side of the house where there was a small, unglazed window, we came in full view of him, seated as coolly as possible beside a bare hearthstone, with a pipe in his mouth and a big brown dog between his knees. His hair, which was snow-white, hung over his shoulders, and his face was browned to the colour of mahogany by exposure to sun and wind; but he might have been carved out of mahogany too for all the sign of attention that he gave while the bailiff repeated his messages, until Kilmoyle, losing patience, tossed a written copy of the notice in to him through the open window, with a threat that, unless he complied with it, he would be smoked out of the place like a rat : after which we rode off, followed by a perfect pandemonium of barks and howls from the dog, a lean and hideous mongrel, who seemed to be only held by force from flying at our throats.

We had a jolly canter over the hills afterwards ; selected the bit of river that seemed most suitable for our fishing on the morrow ; and wound up the day with a couple of bottles of champagne at dinner, after which Kilmoyle was warmed up into making me an offer which I accepted on the spot—*i.e.*, to let me have the identical cottage we had been visiting rent

free, with right of shooting and fishing, for two
years, on condition only of my putting and
keeping it in order for that time. I wonder
what Lily will say to the idea. She hates
Ireland almost as much as Kilmoyle's tenants
are supposed to hate him, but really it would
cost mighty little to make a most picturesque
little place of the cabin in question, and I
believe we should both find it highly enjoy-
able to run down here for a couple of months'
change in the autumn, after a certain and
much-looked-forward-to event is well over.

June 19*th*.—The job is done, and the man
out ; and Kilmoyle and I shook hands laughingly to-day over our victory as he handed me
the key in token of my new tenantship. It
has been rather an exciting bit of work, however ; for the fellow—an ill-conditioned old
villain, who hasn't paid a stiver of rent for
the last twelve months, and only a modicum
for the three previous years—*wouldn't* quit ;

set all threats, persuasions, and warnings at
defiance, and simply sat within his door with
a loaded gun in his hand, and kept it pointed
at anyone who tried to approach him. In
the end, and to avoid bloodshed, we had to
smoke him out. There was nothing else for
it, for though we took care that none of the
neighbours should come near the house with
food, he was evidently prepared to starve
where he was rather than budge an inch ; and
on the third day, Donovan, the bailiff, told
Kilmoyle if he didn't want it to come to that,
he must have in the help either of the 'peelers'
or a bit of smoke.

Kilmoyle vowed he wouldn't have the
peelers anyhow. He had said he'd put the
man out himself, and he'd do it ; and the end
of it was, we first had the windows shuttered
up from outside, a sod put on the chimney,
and then the door taken off its hinges while
the tenant's attention was momentarily dis-

tracted by the former operations. Next, a good big fire of damp weeds which had been piled up outside was set alight, and after that there was nothing to do but wait.

It didn't take long. The wind was blowing strongly in the direction of the house, and the dense volumes of thick, acrid smoke would have driven me out in about five minutes. As for the tenant, he was probably more hardened on the subject of atmosphere generally, for he managed to stand it for nearly half an hour, and until Kilmoyle and I were almost afraid to keep it up lest he should let himself be smothered out of sheer obstinacy. Just as I was debating, however, whether I wouldn't brave his gun, and make a rush in for him at all costs, nature or vindictiveness got the better of his perversity ; a dark figure staggered through the stifling vapour to the door, fired wildly in the direction of Kilmoyle (without hitting him, thank God !), and then dropped, a miserable object, purple with suffocation and black with smoke, upon the threshold, whence one of the keepers dragged him out into the fresh air and poured a glass of whisky down his throat, just too late to prevent his fainting away.

Five minutes later the fire was out, the windows opened, and two stalwart Scotch keepers put in charge of the dwelling, while Kilmoyle and I went home to dinner, and the wretched old man, who had given us so much trouble for nothing, was conveyed in a hand-cart to the village by some of his neighbours, who had been looking on from a distance, and beguiling the time by hooting and groaning at us.

'Who wants the police in these cases?' said Kilmoyle triumphantly. 'To my mind, Glennie, it's mere cowardice to send for those poor fellows to enforce orders we ought to be able to carry out for ourselves, and so get

them into odium with the whole neighbourhood. We managed this capitally by ourselves '—and, upon my word, I couldn't help
agreeing heartily with him. Indeed, the
whole affair had gone off with only one trifling
accident, and that was no one's fault but the
tenant's.

It seems that for the last two days his
abominable dog had been tied up in a miserable little pigsty a few yards from the house,
Donovan having threatened him that if the
brute flew at or bit any one it would be shot
instantly. Nobody was aware of this, however, and unfortunately, when the bonfire was
at its height, a blazing twig fell on the roof of
this little shelter and set it alight; the clouds
of smoke which were blowing that way hiding
what had happened until the wretched animal
inside was past rescue; while even its howls
attracted no attention, from the simple fact
that not only it, but a score of other curs

belonging to the neighbours round, had been making as much noise as they could from the commencement of the affair.

Now, of course, we hear that the evicted tenant goes about swearing that we deliberately and out of malice burnt his only friend alive, and calling down curses on our heads in consequence. I don't think we are much affected by them, however. Why didn't he untie the poor brute himself ? * * *

June 22nd.—A letter from Lady Fitz Herbert, Lily's eldest sister, telling me she thinks I had better come back at once ! L. not at all well, nervous about me, and made more, instead of less, so by my account of our successful raid. What a fool I was to write it ! I thought she would be amused ; but the only thing now is to get back as quickly as possible, and I started this morning, Kilmoyle driving me to the station. We were bowling along pretty fast, when, as we turned a bend

in the road, the horse swerved suddenly to
one side, and the off wheel of the trap went
over something with that sickening sort of
jolt, the meaning of which some of us know
by experience, and which made Kilmoyle
exclaim :

'Good heavens, we've run over something !'

Fortunately nothing to hurt ! Nothing but
the carcase of a dead dog, whose charred and
blackened condition would have sufficiently
identified it with the unlucky victim of
Tuesday's bonfire, even if we had not now
perceived its late owner seated among the
heather near the roadside, and occupied in
pouring forth a string of wailing sounds, which
might have been either prayers or curses for
aught we could tell ; the while he waved his
shaggy white head and brown claw-like hands
to and fro in unison. I yelled at him to
know why he had left his brute of a dog there

to upset travellers, but he paid no attention, and did not seem to hear, and as we were in a hurry to catch the train we could not afford to waste words on him, but drove on. * * *

June 26th. Holly Lodge, West Kensington.— This day sees me the proud father of a son and heir, now just five hours old, and, though rather too red for beauty, a very sturdy youngster, with a fine pair of lungs of his own. Lily says she is too happy to live, and as the dread of losing her has been the one thought of the last twenty-four hours, it is a comfort to know from the doctor that this means she has got through it capitally, and is doing as well as can be expected. Thank God for all His mercies! * * *

July 17th.—Lily has had a nasty fright this evening, for which I hope she won't be any the worse. She was lying on a couch out in the veranda for the first time since her convalescence, and I had been reading to her till she fell asleep, when I closed the book, and, leaving the bell beside her in case she should want anything, went into my study to write letters. I hadn't been there for half an hour, however, when I was startled by a cry from Lily's voice and a sharp ringing of the bell, which made me fling open the study window and dart round to the veranda at the back of the house. It was empty, but in the drawing-room within Lily was standing upright, trembling with terror and clinging to her maid, while she tried to explain to her that there was *someone* hidden in the veranda or close by, though so incoherently, owing to the state of agitation she was in, that it was not till I and the man-servant had searched veranda, garden, and outbuildings, and found nothing, that I was even able to understand what had frightened her.

It appeared then that she had been suddenly awakened from sleep by the pressure of a heavy hand on her shoulder, and a hot breath—so close, it seemed as if someone were about to whisper in her ear—upon her cheek. She started up, crying out, 'Who's that? What is it?' but was only answered by a hasty withdrawal of the pressure, and the pit-pat of heavy but shoeless feet retreating through the dusk to the further end of the veranda. In a sudden access of ungovernable terror she screamed out, sprang to her feet, ringing the bell as she did so, and rushed into the drawing-room, where she was fortunately joined by her maid, who had been passing through the hall when the bell rang.

Well, as I said, we searched high and low, and not a trace of any intruder could we find; nay, not even a stray cat or dog, and we have none of our own. The garden isn't large, and there is neither tree nor shrub in it big enough to conceal a boy. The gate leading into the road was fastened inside, and

the wall is too high for easy climbing ; while
the maid, having been in the hall, could certify
that no one had passed out through the drawing-room.   Finally I came to the conclusion
that the whole affair was the outcome of one
of those very vivid dreams which sometimes
come to us in the semi-conscious moment
between sleep and waking ; and though Lily,
of course, wouldn't hear of such an idea for a
long while, I think even she began to give in
to it after the doctor had been sent for, and
had pronounced it the only rational one, and
given her a composing draught before sending
her off to bed.   At present she is sleeping
soundly, but it has been a disturbing evening,
and I'm glad it's over. * * *

September 20*th.*—Have seen Dr. C—— to-
day, and he agrees with —— that there is
nothing for it but change and bracing air.
He declares that the fright Lily had in July
must have been much more serious than we

imagined, and that she has never got over it.
She *seemed* to do so.   She was out and about
after her confinement as soon as other people;
but I remember now her nerves seemed gone
from the first.   She was always starting,
listening, and trembling without any cause,
except that she appeared in constant alarm
lest something should happen to the baby;
and as I took that to be a common weakness
with young mothers over their first child, I'm
afraid I paid no attention to it.   We've a
very nice nurse for the boy, a young Irish-
woman named Bridget McBean (not that
she's ever seen Ireland herself, but her parents
came from there, driven by poverty to earn
their living elsewhere, and after faithfully
sending over every farthing they could screw
out of their own necessities to ' the ould folks
at home,' died in the same poverty here).
Bridget is devoted to the child, and as long
as he is in her care Lily generally seems easy

and peaceful. Otherwise (and some strange instinct seems to tell her when this is the case) she gets nervous at once, and is always restless and uneasy.

Once she awoke with a scream in the middle of the night, declaring, 'Something was wrong with baby. Nurse had gone away and left it; she was sure of it !' To pacify her I threw on my dressing-gown and ran up to the nursery to see ; and, true enough, though the boy was all right and sound asleep, nurse was absent, having gone up to the cook's room to get something for her toothache. She came back the next moment, and I returned to satisfy Lily, but she would scarcely listen to me.

'Is it *gone ?*' she asked. 'Was the nursery door open? Oh, if it had been ! Thank God, you were in time to drive the thing down. But how—how could it have got into the house ?'

'*It?*   What?' I repeated, staring.

'The dog you passed on the stairs.   I saw it as it ran past the door—a *big black dog!*'

'My dear, you're dreaming.   I passed no dog; nothing at all.'

'Oh, Harry, didn't you see it then?   I did, though it went by so quietly.   Oh, is it in the house still?'

I seized the candle, went up and down stairs and searched the whole house thoroughly; but again found nothing.   The fancied dog must have been a shadow on the wall only, and I told her so pretty sharply; yet on two subsequent occasions when, for some reason or another, she had the child's cot put beside her own bed at night, I was woke by finding her sitting up and shaking with fright, while she assured me that something—*some animal* —had been trying to get into the room.   She could hear its breathing distinctly as it scratched at the door to open it!   Dr. C——

is right. Her nerves are clearly all wrong, and a thorough change is the only thing for her. How glad I am that the builder writes me my Kerry shooting-box is finished ! We'll run over there next week. * * *

September 26*th, The Cabin, Kilmoyle Castle, Kerry.*—Certainly this place is Paradise after London, and never did I imagine that by raising the roof so as to transform a garret into a large, bright attic, quite big enough for a nursery, throwing out a couple of bay windows in the two rooms below, and turning an adjoining barn into a kitchen and servants' room, this cottage could ever have been made into such a jolly little box. As for Lily, she's delighted with it, and looks ever so much better already. Am getting my guns in order for to-morrow, anticipating a pleasant day's shooting:

September 27*th.*—Here's an awful bother ! Bridget has given warning and declares she

will leave to-day! It seems she knew her
mother came from Kerry, and this morning
she has found out that the old man who lived
in this very cottage was her own grandfather,
and that he died of a broken heart within a
week of his eviction, having first called down
a solemn curse on Kilmoyle and me, and all
belonging to us, in this world and the next.
They say also that he managed to scoop out a
grave for his dog, and bury it right in front of
the cabin door; and now Bridget is alternately
tearing her hair for ever having served under
her 'grandfather's murtherer,' and weeping
over the murderer's baby the while she packs
her box for departure. That wouldn't matter
so much, though it's awfully unpleasant; for
the housekeeper at the Castle will send us
someone to mind the boy till we get another
nurse; but the disclosure seems to have
driven Lily as frantic as Bridget. She
entreated me with tears and sobs to give

up the cabin, and take her and baby back to England before 'the curse could fall upon us,' and wept like one brokenhearted when I told her she must be mad even to suggest such a thing after all the expense I have been to. All the same, it's a horrid nuisance. She has been crying all day, and if this fancy grows on her the change will do her no good, and I shan't know what to do. I'm sorry I was cross to her, poor child; but I was rather out of sorts myself, having been kept awake all night by the ceaseless, mournful howling of some unseen cur. Besides, I'm bothered about Kilmoyle. He arranged long ago to be here this week; but the bailiff says he has been ill and is travelling, and speaks in a mysterious way as if the illness were D.T. I hope not! I had no idea before that my old chum was even addicted to drink. Anyhow, I won't be baulked of a few days' shooting, at all events, and perhaps by that time Lily will have calmed down.

    *   *   *   *   *

October 19*th, The Castle.*—It is weeks since I opened this, and I only do so now before closing it for ever. I shall never dare to look at it again after writing down what I must to-day. I did go out for my shooting on the morning after my last entry, and my wife, with the babe in her arms, stood at the cabin door to see me off. The sunlight shone full on them—on the tear-stains still dark under her sweet blue eyes, and the downy head and tiny face of the infant on her breast. But she smiled as I kissed my hand to her. I shall never forget that—the last smile that *ever*. . . . The woman we had brought with us as servant told me the rest. She said her mistress went on playing with the child in the sunshine till it fell asleep, and then laid it in its cot inside, and sat beside it rocking it. By-and-by, however, the maid went in and asked her to come and look at something that was wrong with the new kitchen arrangements, and Lily came out with her. They were in the kitchen about ten minutes, when they heard a wail from the cabin, and both ran out. Lily was first, and cried out :

'Oh, Heaven ! Look ! what's *that*—that great dog. *all black, and burnt-looking*, coming out of the house ? Oh, my baby ! My baby !'

The maid saw no dog, and stopped for an instant to look round for it, letting her mistress run on. Then she heard one wild shriek from within—such a shriek as she had never heard in all her life before—and followed. She found Lily lying senseless on the floor, and in the cradle the child—stone dead ! Its throat had been torn open by some savage animal, and on the bed-clothes

and the fresh white matting covering the
floor were the blood-stained imprints of a
dog's feet !

*   *   *   *   *

That was three weeks ago. It was evening
when I came back ; came back to hear my
wife's delirious shrieks piercing the autumn
twilight — those shrieks which, from the
moment of her being roused from the
merciful insensibility which held her for
the first hours of her loss, she has never
ceased to utter. We have moved her to the
Castle since then ; but I can hear them now.
She has never regained consciousness once.
The doctors fear she never will.

*   *   *   *   *

And she never did ! That last entry in
my diary was written two years ago. For
two years my young wife, the pretty girl
who loved me so dearly, and whom I took
from such a happy home, has been a raving

lunatic—obliged to be guarded, held down, and confined behind high walls. They have been my own walls, and I have been her keeper. The doctors wanted me to send her to an asylum; said it would be for her good, and on that I consented; but she grew so much worse there, her frantic struggles and shrieks for me to come to her, to ' save her from the dog, to keep it off,' were so incessant and heart-rending that they sent for me; and I have never left her again. God only knows what that means; what the horror and agony of those two years, those ceaseless, piteous cries for her child, *our* child; those agonized entreaties to me ' not to go with Kilmoyle; to take her away, away;' those—oh! how have I ever borne it ! . . .

To-day it is over. She is dead; and—I scarce dare leave her even yet ! Never once in all this time have I been tempted to share

the horrible delusion which, beginning in a
weak state of health, and confirmed by the
awful coincidence of our baby's death, upset
my darling's brain; and yet now—now that
it is over, I feel as if the madness which slew
her were coming on me also. As she lay
dying last night, and I watched by her alone,
I seemed to hear a sound of snuffling and
scratching at the door outside, as though some
animal were there.   Once, indeed, I strode to
it and threw it open, but there was nothing—
nothing but a dark, fleeting shadow seen for
one moment, and the sound of soft, unshod
feet going pit, pat, pit, pat, upon the stairs
as they retreated downwards.   It was but
fancy ; my own heart-beats, as I knew ; and
yet —yet if the women who turned me out an
hour ago should have left her alone—if that
sound *now*——

  *   *   *   *   *

Here the writing came to an abrupt end,

the pen lying in a blot across it. At the inquest held subsequently the footman deposed that he heard his master fling open the study door, and rush violently upstairs to the death-chamber above. A loud exclamation, and the report of a pistol-shot followed almost immediately; and on running to the rescue he found Captain Glennie standing inside the door, his face livid with horror, and the revolver in his outstretched hand still pointed at a corner of the room on the other side of the bier, the white covering on which had in one place been dragged off and torn. Before the man could speak, however, his master turned round to him, and exclaiming:

'Williams, *I have seen it!* It was there! *on her!* Better this than a madhouse! There is no other escape,' put the revolver to his head, and fired. He was dead ere even the servant could catch him.

NUMBER TWO, MELROSE SQUARE.

NUMBER TWO, MELROSE SQUARE.

CHAPTER I.

I AM asked to state as clearly as possible why I gave up the house in Melrose Square, Bloomsbury, as suddenly as I did, and what happened there. The landlord says that I have given it a bad name, and prevented him (owing to certain paragraphs which have lately appeared in one of the daily papers) from letting it to another tenant. That is why I have been called upon to make this statement, and I will do so accordingly as briefly and exactly as possible. If the landlord be further hurt by it, I cannot help it. Had I been allowed, I would far rather have avoided ever saying or thinking anything more on the subject. To me it is still an inexpressibly painful one.

I first entered Number Two, Melrose Square, rather late in the afternoon of November 15, 1887; that is, just about a year ago. It was a furnished house taken for me by a friend who was slightly acquainted with the landlord. She had, also on his recommendation, engaged for me a temporary servant, and it was this woman who opened the door for me as I alighted from the cab at it.

She was not a pleasant-looking person; and I remember my first impression of the house was that it looked dark and cheerless, and not so inviting by any means as my friend had described it to me. She, however, had seen it on a bright morning in October, when the sun was shining and the leaves were still ruddy on the trees, while I was entering it under the treble disadvantages of twilight, soaking rain, and a sky low and dense and sooty enough to suggest its being compounded of nothing but exhalations from the river of black mud which lined the streets and made the pavements foul and slippery on every side. No house could look pleasant under such circumstances, and I had not come to London for pleasure, but for hard practical work. I had undertaken the translation of a book which necessitated my constant vicinity to the British Museum for at least six months, and the house in Melrose Square was at once so convenient for the purpose, and so exceedingly—I had almost said ridiculously —low rented that it seemed as though it had been left empty specially for my accommodation. It would have required something more than a little outward dreariness to damp my spirits on my first arrival.

Inside it was rather more cheerful.   The

entrance hall, it is true, was dark and narrow; but Mrs. Cathers, the servant, had lighted a bright fire in the dining-room, and the tea-things were already set out on the table. I began to think that the woman's face belied her character, and that I should not have to suffer from want of attention, at any rate; altogether, I sat down to tea in very good spirits, and afterwards wrote a letter to brother John, with whom I had been staying ever since I let the cottage after our mother's death. It had been a long visit— not too long for him, I hope; but Mrs. John was fussy in her kindness, and would make a visitor of me, and fidget if I shut myself up for an hour with my writing. On the whole I had rather looked forward to being my own mistress again. This evening I did not mean to do anything, however. The journey from the north had been as long and tiring as such journeys always are, and I hardly felt equal to getting out any occupation ; while in the room where I was sitting there was certainly nothing to interest me or amuse my thoughts.

It was a medium-sized apartment, with a rather dingy red Turkey carpet, furniture in the orthodox brown leather and mahogany, and a wall-paper of dull orange striped with maroon.   There were one or two very bad oil-paintings, and an engraving, not at all bad, representing Judas casting down the thirty pieces of silver in the Temple ; a bookcase in one corner, but locked and with no key in it ; and over the chimney-piece a mirror covered with yellow gauze.   I have a particular objec-tion to gilding covered up with yellow gauze anywhere or at any time ; but in this case the glass was covered as well—a precaution as senseless as it was hideous ; and I made up my mind to remove the eye-sore on the morrow.   For that night I was too lazy, and about nine o'clock rang for Mrs. Cathers to bring me my candle that I might go to bed. She went upstairs with me. It was rather a winding staircase, and my bedroom was on the second floor. I had to pass the drawing-room landing, and a window a little way above, just where the stairs took a curve. I remember looking through this window and trying to discover what view it had, and being disappointed because the gloomy blackness of the night without only gave me back a vision of myself reflected in the glass, with Mrs. Cathers' decidedly unprepossessing features a little in my rear. For the moment, indeed, I fancied there were two Mrs. Cathers, or rather a second head a little below hers; but of course that was only a flaw in the glass, and I laughed at myself for the momentary idea that this second head had been more like an old man than my middle-aged servant woman. That is all I recollect of the first night; for after unpacking my trunks I made haste to bed, and slept so soundly that it required more than one knock at my door to arouse me in the morning.

I spent the whole of the next day at the Museum, only returning at dusk to a late dinner. It was still raining then, and the house looked as dreary as it had done on the previous evening. It did not face the square itself—which, indeed, hardly deserved the name, being only a narrow oblong enclosure where a score or so of melancholy trees shook down their last yellow leaves on a wilderness of tall grass and rank weeds, and round which all the houses seemed to have acquired an air of damp and gloom. It opened into a little narrow street turning out of one end of the square, and cut off by iron posts and chains from being a thoroughfare to anywhere; and on that side it was divided from the next house by an archway leading down a long entry to some mews in the rear. The house on the other side, that looking into the square, was empty. So was the one immediately in front, and the big, gaunt letters, ' To Let,' stared me whitely in the face from the dingy windows above and below. It was not a cheerful place ; but, as my friend wrote me, when I asked her to find me nice apartments near the Museum, a furnished house in a square, and with a servant included, for positively less money than you would pay for three rooms in anything like a decent street, was a thing to be grasped at, not despised ; especially as now I could ask Tom and Hester up from their barrack quarters to spend Christmas with me. So I tried to shut my eyes to the exterior look of things and went inside. Here there was one improvement at least—the yellow gauze was gone. I had stripped it off the mirror the last thing before leaving the house in the morning, as also from the glass in the drawing-room, which, though the gilding of the frame was decidedly shabby, was to my great amusement as carefully guarded as the other.

I went up to the latter apartment after dinner. Mrs. Cathers had suggested that ' of course I would not do so, as the dinin'-parlour were so much more cosy ;' but I did not agree with Mrs. Cathers. That orange paper with its maroon stripes, and the grim old engraving of Judas, with the horrible expression of the traitor, and the sinister, leering faces of the high priests and elders, were depressing to my spirits. The very force and realism of the picture made me feel as if the room were one in which it would be possible to plot a crime. Besides, a house in which a drawing-room is unused, except for company, is never a cosy or homelike one to me; and I knew that Hester felt still more strongly on the subject. I was determined that she should find me and my work-basket and books

11

established there as a matter of course when she came.

Neither books nor work were much called into requisition on the present evening, however. There was a pleasant fire burning in the grate, and two candles on the little round table by the sofa, where the last number of the *Cornhill*, with a new novel, lay awaiting my perusal ; but a day's continuous writing and my dinner combined had made me sleepy, and after reading a few pages and finding that I was getting into a dreamy state, and mixing up the crackling of the fire with the roar of surf on a sunny beach, and my own position on the sofa with that of the Scottish heroine in a fast-flying cutter, I gave it up, blew out the candles, and composed myself for a nap till tea-time.

Do these details appear irrelevant to you ? They are not so in reality. I mention them to show you that nothing of what I may afterwards relate can be accounted for (as has been falsely suggested) by my being in an excited, over-wrought state, worked upon by loneliness, or the writing and reading of sensational romances. I was in perfect health. I had lived alone for weeks, and sometimes months, when my dear mother was visiting her married children. I had been simply following my regular profession, which this day lay in the translating a number of dry, scientific, rigidly matter-of-fact letters, had walked home, eaten a plain dinner, and read myself comfortably to sleep with a description of sea-coast scenery by one of our healthiest and most bracing English writers. Bear this in mind as I wish you to do, and then listen to what follows.

I woke from my nap with a start, caused by the falling of a coal into the fender. How long I had slept I could not tell; but I had that instinctive consciousness, which I dare

say most people have experienced, that it was
a long time, much longer than I had intended;
and this opinion was confirmed by the sight
of the tea-things standing on the table, where
Mrs. Cathers had evidently placed them without rousing me, and also by the fact that
when I touched the teapot I found it was
almost stone-cold.   Vexed with myself, I rose
quickly to my feet and began putting the fire
together; for it had got so low and dead that
the room was almost dark.   Indeed, I feared
at first that there was not sufficient vitality in
it to light a candle, and so enable me to see
what time it was, and whether it was worth
while beginning any occupation; but a few
skilful touches with the poker soon dispelled
this idea and produced a bright, wavering
flame; and I stood up again, meaning to get
a spill from the mantelpiece and light it at it.
As I did so, my glance naturally fell on my
own face in the mirror before me, and I said

to myself aloud, and smiling as one sometimes will when alone :

'Well, Miss Mary Liddell, you have made your head into a furze-bush ! It's a mercy Mrs. John isn't here to see you, or——'

My voice broke off suddenly at that word ; for in the act of uttering it, and smiling to myself at my dishevelledness, as I have said, I saw that I was not alone in the room.

Standing at the farther end of it, almost opposite to the grate, and reflected in the mirror by the ruddy light, was a woman; a woman I had never seen before. That she had not been there five minutes back when I awoke I could almost have sworn ; for I had looked all round the room ; and dim as the light was, I could see well enough that there was no one else in it, and that the door was closed. It was closed now, and how she could have opened and shut it again without my hearing her, unless during the moment that I was poking the fire, I could not imagine. The curious thing was that she did not look at or speak to me even now; but stood perfectly still, her face turned towards the door as if in the attitude of listening, and with all the appearance of a person belonging to the house, seeing that she was not dressed for walking, but in a loose sort of morning gown of white cambric, with deep ruffles down the front and at the wrists, and wore her hair loosely plaited down the back.   I noticed this at the first glance as adding to the strangeness of her presence there at all; but in the same moment the fire shot up in a brilliant flame, throwing a bright light on her face, and almost nailing me to the ground as my eyes read the expression on it.   In all the years I have lived, in all the years I may yet have before me, I never have seen, I trust I never may see, such an expression on any human being's face again !   For it was a young face—that of a girl, almost a child ; and would have been pretty but for the awful, corpse-like pallor which overshadowed the brow and cheeks, and the hopeless, unutterable depth of misery, of utter despair, and helpless, speechless, livid horror, all blended in one single effort, an intensity of listening, which seemed to absorb every nerve and power ; listening to some-thing *outside the door*, something which seemed from her starting eyeballs and the hopeless quiver in her lower jaw to be draw-ing nearer and nearer ; for her slender, feeble body seemed to shrink with each breath, and draw itself farther and farther back, as though from some loathsome, terrible animal, which she could see in act to spring, or as though—— It was all visible in the sudden leaping up of that flame. The next moment it died down again, and I turned round sharply !

The woman was gone !

How I felt I cannot tell you. It has taken many words to write all this, but it did not require the space of one minute to see it. It must have taken you many seconds to read, but it did not take a dozen heart-beats to feel it in all its ghastly, inexplicable mystery. I was still breathless with the surprise of seeing her there—there in my room, which only a moment before had been empty save of myself; and she was gone—disappeared! The door had not opened. There was no sound, no cry, not even the lightest footfall. The house seemed wrapped in the most impenetrable silence. Even the noises in the street were hushed; and I was there alone in the firelight with the unlit spill in my hand. I suppose I rang the bell violently; for I remember listening to the sound of it jingling far away in the basement regions, and then ringing it again and again, and waiting, with my heart beating like an alarum-clock, and my hands quite cold and damp, for Mrs. Cathers to answer it.

. She made her appearance at last. It may not have been as long as it seemed. One does not tell time accurately at such moments; but it was long enough to give me leisure to recover myself a little, and to feel annoyed with the woman for the marked sullenness and unwillingness in her whole manner as she entered with the conventional query : ' Did you ring, ma'am ?' She was carrying a large kerosene lamp, and the sudden glare of light, as well as the sound of her voice, surly as it was, restored me further.

' I should think you heard me ring several times,' I answered. ' Did you meet anyone on the stairs just now ? I have been asleep longer than I intended, and I did not hear the door open ; but——'

' Yes, ma'am, you 'ave been asleep,' Mrs. Cathers interrupted me in a tone of greater

injury than before. 'And if I didn't answer
of your bell the minnit it ringed, it was in
cause of my bein' that tired of waitin' up I'd
dropt into a doze myself a-sittin' in my cheer.
P'r'aps, ma'am, you don't know as it's twelve
o'clock?'

'Twelve o'clock!' I repeated.   Had I
really slept so long? 'Why did you not
wake me when you brought up the tea?' I
added, looking at the woman in surprise.

'Why, m'm,' she said peevishly, 'I would
have done so, in course, if you 'adn't said at
dinner as you were tired; an' when I come
up you were sleepin' so sound I didn't like.
Dreamin' I should think you was too, by your
'air,' the woman put in with a sudden furtive
glance at me.

I had not been able to catch her eyes once
before. She kept them rigidly fixed on the
lamp she carried, never even looking about
her; and, indeed, there was something now

so unpleasant in her glance, that I felt almost unwilling to go on speaking to her. Still, if anyone had got into the house without my knowledge—anyone of feeble mind, or in great terror! Writing this as though I were in the witness-box, I can solemnly aver that so free was my mind from any morbid or romantic fancies that, even then, I could not think of my visitor as having any supernatural element.

'Have you let anyone into the house without my knowing?' I asked, rather sharply. 'Or is the hall-door open? If you have been asleep yourself, you might not hear anyone come in at it; but I believe someone did just now—a woman. She was in this room a few minutes ago.'

Mrs. Cathers looked at me again, this time with barely veiled contempt.

'You 'ave been dreamin', ma'am!' she said coolly. 'The 'all door! Why, it 'ave been

shut an' locked ever since dusk, an' as to me
lettin' anyone in, I'd not think of such a
thing. There ain't no one in this 'ouse but
you and me ; nor there hasn't been, man or
woman either. Lor', to think what queer
dreams some folks 'ave ! But I thought as
you were give that way, when I 'eard you
mumbling to yourself in your sleep.'

I did not believe her, for I knew that I had
not been dreaming ; and there was something
in the woman's whole manner which made me
distrustful of her, and more especially of her
almost impertinent determination to force a
ready-made solution of my query on me.
Why should she be so anxious to persuade me
that I had been dreaming, when, as a matter
of fact, she could have no idea of my grounds
for speaking as I did ? On second thoughts,
I decided to say no more on the subject at
present ; but, simply observing that she
ought to have woke me sooner, told her to

light me up to bed, and make haste to her own. I could not have stayed longer just then in that drawing-room by myself, and I am perfectly willing to own that until I was safely in bed, with my room-door locked, I avoided looking about me as carefully as Mrs. Cathers had done. I was honestly frightened and bewildered, and my mind was in a whirl. It was a comfort to me when three, striking from a church-clock hard by, and followed by the crowing of an over-wakeful cock, showed me that the actual night was past, and gave me confidence enough to let me sleep.

The following day, the 17th of November, was bright and sunny; and I awoke, feeling more cheerful, and able to reason with myself quite calmly as to the last night's occurrence. Looking back upon it thus, through the medium of sunlight and a refreshing sleep, I could only conclude that, however unlikely and foreign to all my previous experience, I had simply been the victim of some strange optical delusion, though how produced, and whence arising, I could not tell. Against any other idea, that, for instance, which had already presented itself to me, of some mad or imbecile girl being concealed in the house with Mrs. Cathers' connivance, I guarded by looking into every room and cupboard immediately after breakfast, and, after locking up those which I did not require for present occupation, depositing the keys in my desk.

I spent the greater part of that day, like the last, at the British Museum, and afterwards called on some old friends in Russell Place, and stayed to dinner with them. I had been half in hopes of carrying off one of the girls to spend a few days with me, for the strange vividness and reality of the last night's vision, and the sense of horror and mystery encompassing it, had left a sufficiently strong

impression on me still to make me wishful for
some other company than my own. I was
not exactly afraid to be alone, but my nerves
had received an unpleasant shock, and I
wished to assist myself to recover from it. I
was disappointed, however, both the daughters
being away on a visit in the country; but
their father, one of the kindest and most
genial men living, insisted on seeing me home
at night, and even came in and sat for half
an hour or so talking to me, greatly, as I
judged from her face, to the discontent of Mrs.
Cathers. Indeed, the sourness of her expression, when she saw me return accompanied by
a clergyman, even attracted the old gentleman's attention, and caused him to observe
laughingly to me :

' Why, Mary, my dear, one would think
you were a jealous wife, with a husband
partial to pretty servant-girls, and had chosen
the most repellent you could find accordingly.

Does your Abigail always present such an unamiable appearance ?'

She was to have her amiability further tried. My kind friend, to whom I had half-jestingly mentioned the previous night's fright, insisted on looking over the house with me before he left, so as to 'set my mind at rest,' he said; and Mrs. Cathers resented the proceeding so much that she came up to me in the middle of it, and, without taking any notice of Mr. L——'s presence, asked me, in her strongest tone of ill-usage, whether I objected to her going to bed, ' seeing as how it were past twelve before she got to rest last night, and just on eleven now, and having been hard at work since——'

I told her shortly that she might go to bed as soon as she pleased. When you are used to nice old family servants with gentle, respectful ways, this sort of coarse incivility grates on you, and as I bid my kind old friend good-night, a few minutes later, I told him, smiling:

'Well, I think I shall take your advice in one respect before Tom and Hester come, although she is rather a jealous wife. I shall look out for a pleasanter maid.'

I said this with the hall-door in my hand— he will bear witness now how cheerfully, and how little the thought that I should never require another maid in that house, or sleep another night there, had occurred to me. Indeed, I can safely say that such an idea had never been further from my mind. I went back to the dining-room quite cheerfully too. Originally, I had intended going to bed very early, and had even, by an impulse which I was ashamed to put into words, re-covered the mirror with its hideous yellow veil; but the evening with my cheery-hearted friends had so restored my natural spirits that I felt divided between laughter and blushes at

12

my own folly in so doing, and, finding a little pile of letters and proofs which had come for me by the last post lying on the side-table, I sat down to look over them, and speedily got so absorbed in the task as to forget altogether how time was passing.

I was aroused from it quite suddenly by a feeling which I cannot explain, but yet which was strong enough to make me lift my head with a start, and look sharply around: a feeling that someone was in the same room with me!

CHAPTER II.

I SAID at the end of the last chapter that I was aroused from my occupation by the sensation that someone was in the room with me. It was not so in fact. One glance round the formal gas-lit apartment, with its rather skimpy curtains looped flatly against the wall, and its utter absence of anything like dark corners or ghostly recesses, was enough to assure me of my error; but the feeling remained with me all the same, and grew stronger instead of passing away. It almost seemed as though someone were seated at the same table with me, breathing near me, occupying the very next chair; and then gradually there stole over me the same sensation I had had before with regard to this room, as if some crime, some deadly, sickening sin which appalled me even while I was utterly ignorant of its nature, were being plotted and worked out in it—something too hideous to be rendered into words, but to which I, by the very fact of my presence there, was being made a party. It was then, at that moment, that the thought of what I had seen in the mirror last night came into my mind. I was exactly under the drawing-room floor where *it* had stood—the vision woman with that awful mystery of horror and despair in her livid cheeks, and dim, dilated eyes. Was this unknown, unguessed-at wickedness being woven and worked out against *her?* Was she up there now, waiting ?

I had been sitting down, holding my letters in my hand, trying honestly and hard to think of them and nothing else. I could not do so any longer. I stood up abruptly. There was a trembling in my limbs and hands, and my forehead felt cold and moist. All the while I was putting up my papers my eyes would keep wandering by a sort of fascination to the mirror. I could see nothing in it. The gauze prevented me; yet it seemed to me more than once as if the reflection of something—some moving figure, not mine, had passed across it; as if, but for the veil—— I could not bear it, and went out quickly from the room, shutting and locking the door behind me. There was no light in the hall or upon the stairs, except the candle I carried. After putting that ready for me, Mrs. Cathers had turned out the gas. I went upstairs with swift steps; swiftest in passing the drawing-room door.

I have said the staircase took a bend here and crossed a long window, which in daylight lighted it from top to bottom. This window gave onto the dead wall of a neighbouring house about eight feet distant. There was no blind to it. As on the first night, it frowned on me in black, unsheltered nakedness when I turned the corner. As on the first night, I saw myself reflected at full length in it, the candle in my hand, the buttons and fringes of my dress, the—— My God! but *who*, who or *what* was that behind me, that crouching figure which froze me to the spot, actually paralyzed with dread—a dread which was all the more overmastering because I had heard no faintest rustle or sound to give me warning of it!

Believe me or not; but just below me, creeping slowly with soft, gliding, noiseless steps, was the figure of a man!

At the moment he was not on the same angle of the stairs with me. The banisters separated us, and at first the light only fell on his head: the head of an old man, bald, with tufts of grayish white hair hanging in coarse,

shaggy locks over the large, red, wrinkly ears,
and a short, stubbly beard, white too : an old
man with stooping shoulders and heavily-
corrugated brow. The face beneath was inexpressibly evil and repulsive ; evil and repulsive in the loose, hanging, sensual lips ;
evil and repulsive in the cruel, vindictive eyes
almost hidden under their overhanging brows ;
so evil and repulsive in every line and curve
of the hoary head and brutal, wolfish jaws,
that even if met by daylight in a crowded
street one would instinctively have shuddered
and shrunk away from contact with him.
How much more so now, when illumined by
an expression of such deadly, sinister determination that the very sight of it seemed to
chill one's heart and limbs, and deprive one
even of the power of a cry for help !

In that moment of mortal, agonized terror,
longer in seeming than all the years of my
past life, I felt as though in the presence of

some ferocious animal—some creature without pity, without conscience, without soul, whose very glance must foul and destroy if it once fell on one.

For that was the strangest part of it, adding in one way to the mystery and horror of his presence. This creature, this man, never looked at me; seemed (if it were possible to believe such a thing) unconscious even of my presence. Like the vision-woman of last night, its eyes were fixed straight before it. Like the vision-woman's of last night, they never blinked or wandered once, but seemed concentrated in one fixed, deadly stare; a stare which had for its object the drawing-room door! Could it be—was it possible, or was this some horrible, fevered dream?—that she was there *now*, cowering behind the door; a woman, young, almost a child, alone in the night, utterly friendless, utterly helpless, waiting and listening in an anguish of fear beyond words, beyond hope, beyond even prayer, for the approach of this very man who, step by step, was gradually drawing nearer to her—the man whose unseen presence had made the room below horrible with meditated crime: whom I had thought to leave behind me there !

I could see the whole of him now. Inch by inch, with a stealthy, crawling movement, as though he were raising himself by the wrinkled, sinewy hand, which grasped the rail of the banisters so close to me that it almost touched my dress, rather than by the use of his feet, he had gained the landing outside the drawing-room door; and I saw that he was clad only in trousers and shirt—the latter open at the throat so as to show the wrinkled, hairy skin; also that he carried in his left hand an ordinary table-knife with a black horn handle, the blade of which, worn to a point like a dagger, had evidently been recently sharpened. I saw, too, for the first time, that he was not alone. Close to his side, and alternately rubbing herself against his legs and the knuckles of his left hand, was a big, yellow, gaunt-bodied cat, with an unusually large head, and one eye bleeding and sore from some recent wound. There was something peculiarly horrible about this cat, horrible even in the almost obtrusive way in which she lavished her caresses on her sinister companion, and then, leaping forward, crouched down at the door, smelling at it and turning her sound eye on her master as if aware of his object and inviting him to hurry with it. Still without a word, and seeming indeed to hold his breath between his clenched teeth, he struck at her with the knife to drive her off; and then, gliding closer to the door, gave one furtive glance around him, and tightening his hold of the weapon, laid his hand upon the lock.

That broke the spell which held me, and had held me till then, numb and speechless; and as the handle slowly turned under those cruel, sinewy fingers I shrieked aloud, shrieked again and again, till the whole house rang with my cries of fear and horror; shrieked, and springing wildly forward, saw——*nothing!* a blank, empty space, where a moment before had been man and animal, and let the candle fall out of my nerveless fingers down between the banister and far below, clattering into the darkness.

  *   *   *   *   *

What happened next, or how I got there, I shall never know; but it was early dawn when I recovered consciousness, and I was lying face downwards on the floor in my own room. Someone—Mrs. Cathers it was—was trying to lift me up; but at first I did not recognise her, and the touch of a hand only wrung a faint cry from me, and made me go

off again into a second fainting-fit. I suppose she must have got some water then and
dashed it in my face; for, when I next revived,
both it and my hair were dripping with wet,
and I opened my eyes and saw her bending
over me. But I was still only half-conscious.
I did not know where I was or what had
happened to me; and my first effort of returning life was to cling to this woman, so repug-
nant to me usually, and moan out faint con-
tradictory entreaties that she would stay with
me; that she would not leave me; and then,
at the same time, that she would run to that
poor girl and save her. 'Oh, do go to her;
do, *do*, or he will kill her! He will have
killed her by now.'

'Killed her! Why, ma'am, whatever are
you talking on? There's no one in the 'ouse
but you an' me. There ain't, indeed. On
my conscience there ain't.'

This, or something like this, Mrs. Cathers

kept repeating ; but I hardly heard or understood.   The frenzy of terror, only half sub-
dued by exhaustion, was still on me ; and
when I found she would not move I tried to
rise, and failing, burst into a fit of hysterical
weeping, which lasted so long that Mrs.
Cathers got quite frightened.   She ran for
some brandy and poured it down my throat,
and this partially revived me ; but by that
time I was as weak as a child, and the woman
had to half lift, half drag me on to the bed,
and then stoop her head low to hear my
whispered request, urged with tremulous
eagerness, that even if she were sure that
there was no one in the house, she would
send at once to the friends I had been with
last evening, and beg Mrs. L—— to come to
me.   To my surprise and sorrow, however,
this Mrs. Cathers would not do.   She had a
hundred reasons to the contrary.   There was
no one to send, and I was not well enough to

be left, and if I liked to write to Mrs. L——
later she would put the note in the pillar ; all
of which did not satisfy me; for with my
suspicions of the woman revived by her reluctance to carry out such a simple and natural
wish, I could not feel sure that any letter I
might write would reach its destination.
Besides, a better idea had come into my head,
and finding her obstinate on that score, I
begged her to help me to dress, and call a
cab, declaring that I would go to the L——'s
myself.   That would save all delay, and they
would take care of me.   I could not and would
not sleep another night in that house.

Mrs. Cathers lost patience.

'Tush, ma'am !   What's the matter with
the 'ouse ?' she said rudely, and pressed me
back on the pillows with a hand strong enough
to be unpleasantly suggestive in my weakened
state.   'There's not a soul stirred in it but
yourself after· the gentleman went last night,

and nothing ain't happened, excep' that you've nearly druv yourself into a fever, an' got a fit of the hysterics with the bad air in that beastly Museum, and writin' mornin', noon, an' evenin', too, as is enough to drive anyone mad. I expect you was reg'lar wore out, and most like fell asleep aside of your bed a-sayin' your prayers, and got awful night-mares in consequence, as was only natural. Why, you was cryin' out and struggling in one still when I came upstairs. And now just you lie down, ma'am, an' take a sleep to quiet you. Why, bless you! you'll be all right when you wake, and thankful to me I didn't let you go rampagin' about when you wasn't sensible what you was sayin' or doin'.'

I looked up in the woman's face and saw that it was useless to try either argument or command on her; for there was a darkly obstinate expression about her mouth which told me she meant to have her way. Perhaps if I pretended to give in to her, and lay still for a while, I might be able to get up later and leave the house without any further appeal to her.   That any such appeal would be futile I felt sure.   Indeed, her resoluteness in keeping me in the house and preventing me from speaking to other people, with her peculiarly persistent avoidance of asking me any question, either now or on the previous night, as to what had happened, preferring to put forward instead a made-up story of her own, as though she were going through a programme learnt by rote beforehand, made me certain that she either knew more of the secrets of this gloomy house than anyone suspected, or was in the landlord's pay to keep them from being brought to the light of day at any cost, even of life or reason, to a tenant. Put before yourself what would be the natural curiosity, wonder, and sympathy of most women of the lower orders on such an occasion, and I think you will come to a similar conclusion.

Acting on this idea, I made believe to yield to her way of thinking, and also to her making me a cup of tea, which she declared would do me all the good in the world. In truth I was both thirsty and anxious above all things to regain strength enough to carry out my purpose ; and, therefore, when she brought me up a large breakfast-cup full, I raised myself and drank it off greedily, although it struck me in so doing that it was not good tea, and had a strange bitter flavour. The next moment I felt myself sinking heavily back and my eyes closing. I opened them with an effort, and looked at Mrs. Cathers. There was a smile on her face ; but it seemed to be getting fainter, as though I saw it through a thickening mist ; and when I tried to say, ' You have given me a narcotic,' my voice sounded thick, and the words seemed to

lose themselves between my teeth.   Before
they were fairly uttered, sound and sight, too,
had faded away, and I was fast asleep.

How long I slept I do not know, but I
should judge it was about four hours.   Nar-
cotics, especially in strong doses, have rather
a curious effect on me.   They both operate
and lose their power far more rapidly and
thoroughly than with most people.   It wanted
a few minutes to eleven when I awoke, and,
with the exception of a slight headache, I felt
at once that both my perceptions and my
memory were quite clear.   My bodily powers,
too, had come back in a great degree ; for,
though I felt much weaker than usual, I was
quite able to rise, and lost no time in dressing
myself for walking, and in putting up my
money and a few valuables in a small hand-
bag as softly and swiftly as possible.   My
intention was to leave the house, if possible
without seeing Mrs. Cathers again ; and at

first I seemed likely to succeed. There was no sign of her on the stairs as I passed that awful window, now blank and bare, and filled with raw, white daylight; or in the drawing-room, the door of which stood wide open; and as I hastened down a shudder ran through my limbs, and a feeling of sickness came over me, when I noticed, what I had not seen before, a large brownish stain, only partially obliterated by scraping and washing, on the stencilled wall just inside the room.

There was no sign of Mrs. Cathers in the hall either, and the whole house was as still and silent as if she too had dosed herself off to sleep. It was, therefore, an unpleasant shock to me when I lifted the latch of the front door, expecting next moment to be in the street, to find that it was locked and the key gone. The dining-room, too, was in darkness, the shutters being still up and barred; and a feeling of nervous dread prevented me

from giving more than a hasty glance into it.
I preferred to boldly invade the kitchen
regions, and, if I saw Mrs. Cathers, desire
her to let me out by the area door. She
could hardly refuse ; and if she did, there
were enough passers-by at this time for me
to easily attract someone's attention. I went
downstairs accordingly. They were narrow
stairs, and, though clean enough at present,
had evidently not been kept so by previous
tenants, for they were stained with blackish
spots and patches nearly all the way to the
bottom, as though something had been spilt
down them, and, soaking into the wood,
remained there. I noticed too that the wall
on one side had been whitewashed for about
three feet up at a much later period than the
rest.

To my surprise Mrs. Cathers was not in
the kitchen below ; nor in her own room,
which adjoined it, and the door of which

stood open, showing me that her bonnet and shawl were gone from the peg where, on my previous visits to the basement, I had always seen them hanging.   It flashed upon me then that she had gone out on some errand of her own, trusting to my being sound asleep, and probably meaning to return before the influence of the narcotic had worn off; and when, to my intense relief and thankfulness, I discovered that she had omitted or forgotten to fasten the area door behind her, I felt as though a heavy weight had been rolled off my heart, and a sudden resolution came to me to profit by her absence by endeavouring to discover some clue, if any existed, to those horrors nightly enacted upstairs.   It did not seem likely that I should; but at least I had courage to try.

The kitchen and lower offices generally I had examined before, and found them all alike, dreary in the dreariness of a dark November day, rather bare and very clean.   Mrs. Cather's room remained ; but that came under the same category.   There was not even anything lying about in it.   She kept all her possessions in a small trunk, which was locked.   There was no looking-glass in the room ; and the key was inside the door.   Did she fasten herself in at night, and remain so, unmoved by any shrieks or cries for help from upstairs ?   There was nothing to be learnt here.

I had only one more place to visit, a small yard at the back of the house.   Originally, perhaps, it had been a garden ; for there were a couple of lilac-bushes and a holly at one end of it ; but these had evidently not borne a leaf for years, and being coated with a thick garment of soot, stood up against the dank, mildewed walls like black spectres.   They were high walls, so high that even if there had been any sun it could hardly have forced an entrance; and the ground beneath was black, too, and sodden with moisture. At one side there was a huge tub for rain-water, and a pile of old bottles; at the bottom a worm-eaten, tumbling-to-pieces summer-house. That was all. I do not know what took my steps to the last-named place. Standing there under the low leaden sky, and half hidden by the spectral lilac-bushes, it presented an appearance even more gloomy, sinister, and desolate than the rest; yet something within me, something which I could not resist, seemed to force me to the door and compel me to look inside. There was nothing to be seen there at first—nothing, at least, but a pile of wood heaped up on one side, and a rusty old chopper lying across some of the billets, with which Mrs. Cathers had evidently been chopping them up for her fire; but as I stood gazing, something living seemed to move at one end of the woodstack; and to my

unutterable horror—a horror which must have
been felt to be understood—there came out a
large yellow cat, very gaunt and rough-
skinned, with an unusually big head and only
one eye.

For the moment I thought I should have
fainted again. This animal, hideous in itself,
and the very facsimile of that whose horrible
gambols I had witnessed the previous night,
seemed like a part of that ghastly scene risen
up again in proof of its reality; and for a
minute or so the walls of the building seemed
to swim round with me, and I was forced to
lean on the wood-stack to save myself from
falling. Then I saw that the ground where
the animal had been crouching was hollowed
into a hole, partly by her own claws, partly,
perhaps, by chopping billets on it; and at
the present moment she had returned there,
and was licking and growling over a bone,
which, from its whiteness and the earth on

one end of it, appeared to have been disinterred
in the process.   It was a very small bone,
not bigger than that in a rabbit's fore-leg or a
human finger; and close by I saw a gleam of
something else, also white, showing through
the loosened mould.   Conquering my repugnance, I stooped down, and with a shrinking
beyond all words, and which gives me a sick
feeling now to think of it, drew out this white
thing, discovering it to be a second bone
resembling the first.   A few blackish fibres
like threads were hanging from it, and to it a
fragment of stuff—muslin, apparently—was
adhering.

The cat lay still, watching me all the while
with her one vicious eye, and growling
furtively.   With an involuntary gesture of
disgust I dropped the bone almost as soon as
I had touched it, but the bit of muslin had
got caught on my finger, and obliged me to
look at it more closely.   It was a scrap of

cambric about nine inches long and two broad, hemmed at one side and gathered at the other, like a frill or ruffle ; but it had evidently been torn roughly from the article of dress to which it belonged, and one end was stained with some dark brown liquid, which had dried and caked it into a hard, crumpled mass.

Like a frill or ruffle! Like—like—good God ! was it only a fancy ?—the ruffles at *her* wrist ; and stained with——

How I left that horrible house I hardly know ; but five minutes later I was outside it in the open street, and I have never entered it again. For several weeks I lay very ill in Russell Place ; so ill that Hester was sent for from Aldershot to help the L——'s in nursing me ; and as soon as I was well enough to be moved she took me back there with her, and afterwards returned with me to the North, where I have remained quietly almost ever since. On the second day of my illness Mrs. L—— and my brother-in-law went to the house in Melrose Square. Mrs. Cathers was there, and opened the door to them, professing great alarm at my absence and entire innocence as to the possibility of anything in the house being the occasion of it; but when she found that one of their first objects was to summarily send her about her business her manner altered, and she sturdily refused to go, declaring that she had been put into the house by the other lady and the landlord, and that no one had any right to send her off at a moment's warning because a poor, weak-minded lady had got a fever. She had done all she could for her, and tried to keep her quietly in bed; though as to drugging her, that was all an invention, and she would swear she had not. Let them take her to a magistrate and try; and if the poor, silly woman would get up and go out, what could be expected but that she would get worse ? Why, she had seen at the very beginning what a nervous, hysterical state she was in ; and had told the landlord she did not much like being alone with such a person ; and the least she expected was a month's board and wages in compensation. Tom had written to the landlord already, and an angry interview and correspondence ensued ; the latter gentleman persisting in treating all suspicion of there being anything wrong in the house as equally childish and insulting, insisting on having the ground of the summer-house dug up, and triumphantly pointing out that there was nothing buried there (this was a week after my visit to the spot, and who could tell what had been done in the interim ?), while he spoke of me uniformly as a poor, nervous bibliomaniac, worked up into a brain-fever by a disordered digestion and an over-wrought brain. Indeed, he even threatened to claim a quarter's rent, declaring that the house had been taken for six months ; but my brother-in-law fought this valiantly, and he had to be content with the month's rent he had received in advance.

As to Mrs. Cathers, she disappeared during the quarrel between her superiors, and was heard of no more. My firm belief is, and always will be, that she was aware of the evil character of the house, and was heavily paid by the landlord to act as servant to his tenants in it, and cast a slur on anything they might declare they had seen there. He, of course, spoke of her as a person of the highest character, and pointed to the fact that none of my property had been disturbed in my absence as proof thereof.

But what was the explanation of the mystery ? What was the dark secret of this house, so strangely and horribly shadowed forth to me ? After minute inquiries among the neighbours and shopkeepers in the vicinity, I can only say I do not know! The mystery is still unexplained, the secret still hidden in those dreary walls, never probably to be unveiled on earth. All that Mrs. L——— and the lawyer, acting for me, could find out in their research was this: The house had been untenanted for a year and a half before I took it, the last people who lived there being a blind old lady with her husband and two servants. The aged couple used to go to bed very early, and the servants slept downstairs, and never spoke of having heard or seen anything out of the common; but one night the husband, having to come downstairs for his wife's medicine, must have missed his footing, for he was heard falling to the bottom, and was picked up speechless and dying. The blind widow went away after that, and the household broke up.

Who had the house before them? Oh, a young couple; but they only stayed a week or so, and left suddenly. Reported in the neighbourhood that the landlord turned them out ; said they were not respectable people.

And before that ? Before that it had been empty a good while, ever since the old gentleman lived there who owned it and was uncle to the present landlord. Married ? No ; nor likely to have been ; a very ill-favoured old gent, and not pleasant in his manners either. Had a ward living with him, however—a young lady ; but she was said to be a sad invalid, never went out, and no one ever saw her, except now and then at an upper window. They went away all in a hurry to France— indeed, no one knew of it till they were gone ; for they were not sociable people, only kept one servant, latterly a charwoman, who did not sleep in the house, and had no acquaintances in the neighbourhood. Folks said the young lady died abroad, and perhaps her guardian found the house lonesome without her; for though he came back after a time he did not stay. Anyhow, he was dead, too, now; for that was how the house came to the present owner, who had never lived there himself, but let it just as it stood, furnished.

Dead! And there was an end of the clue, if any had existed. It could be traced no farther. Probably it never will be now, since, as I have said, the man and his ward are both dead; though how she died, or where, no one will ever know save God, who looks down on all the ghastly secrets of this earth and suffers them to lie hidden in His hand until the Day of Judgment. Anyhow, the house is there now, empty. You may pass it any day and read the big 'To Let' in sprawling letters on a card in the dining-room window. No one has ever opened the shutters in that dreary room. A rumour has got about that Number Two is haunted, and that evil sights are seen

there ; and the landlord cannot let it in consequence.   That is why he is now threatening
me with an action for libel ; and if he chooses
he may, of course, carry it out.   In my
defence I can only make a plain statement,
the same that I have written here.   Let
anyone else make what further examination
he pleases, and draw his own conclusions.